"Did you think I was going to take you to some ho-tel, mo-tel Holiday Inn?

"You should know me better than that. You only get the best, baby. And I didn't want to keep our neighbors up since I think you're gonna be loud."

She opened her mouth for an indignant retort and got a mouthful of joy for her efforts. He covered her lips with his and kissed her until she was breathless. "I'm not loud," she whispered.

"Yes, but you will be." Still holding her hips, he pulled her closer, stroking and squeezing her butt. "Did I ever tell you what a cute bottom you have?"

"Actually, no, you've never mentioned it."

MELANIE SCHUSTER

started reading when she was four, and believes that's why she's a writer today. She was always fascinated with books and loved telling stories. From the time Melanie was very small she wanted to be a writer. She fell in love with romance novels when she began reading the ones her mother would bring home. She would go to any store that sold paperbacks and load up! Whenever Melanie had a spare moment she was reading. She loves romance fiction because it's always so hopeful. Despite the harsh realities of life, romance stories always remind readers of the wonderful, exciting adventure of falling in love and meeting your soul mate. Melanie believes in love and romance with all her heart. She finds fulfillment in writing stories about compelling couples who find true, lasting love in the face of all the obstacles out there. She hopes all of her readers find true love. If they've already been lucky enough to find love, Melanie hopes that they never forget what it felt like to fall in love.

A
Case for
Romance

MELANIE
SCHUSTER

KIMANI
ROMANCE

This one is for all my readers. You have encouraged me
in good times and lifted me up during bad times and
I appreciate every one of you. Stay blessed and keep
reading, the best is yet to come.

 KIMANI PRESS™

Recycling programs
for this product may
not exist in your area.

ISBN-13: 978-0-373-86098-2
ISBN-10:   0-373-86098-6

A CASE FOR ROMANCE

Copyright © 2009 by Melanie Schuster

www.kimanipress.com

Printed in U.S.A.

Dear Reader,

So many of you wanted to know if I was going to write about Ayanna finding love that I was glad I planned this story. Ayanna has been a dedicated mother for so long she's forgotten all about being a woman. And when her beloved boys spend the summer with her mom in South Carolina, she has the perfect opportunity to have a little fun. She feels comfortable with Johnny Phillips because he's the brother of her best friend. But he very quickly lets her know that he's attracted to her in a very non-brotherly fashion. Their dating turns into a steamy affair that Ayanna assumes is just for the summer. Johnny doesn't have any plans for ending their romance, ever.

I always like books in which the player gets caught up in his own game, and this is a variation on that. Johnny has always vowed that he would never get married, ever. But he can't make that claim anymore; there's something about Ayanna that has him sprung, totally caught up. The fact that she's not taking their relationship as seriously as he is is a real wake-up call for him.

It's not that Ayanna doesn't have strong feelings for Johnny—she does. But she decides to get from him what she can, while she can. With Ayanna it's a case of not getting her feelings hurt by not getting her hopes up.

I wanted to explore the idea that there are two big obstacles that can prevent you from getting what you want out of life. Sometimes, like Johnny, you don't really know what you want, and sometimes, like Ayanna, you don't think you can have it because you believe it's out of your league.

What I have found is that you can make your wishes come true if you're smart enough to know the deepest desire of your heart and you're bold enough to go after it.

Stay Blessed,
Melanie

I Chronicles 4:10
MelanieAuthor@aol.com

Acknowledgments

To Gwen Osborne, Janice Sims and my sister
Betty Dowdell for always being there for me.
Your positive thoughts and prayers always sustain me.
A special shout-out to Jan, who keeps me laughing.

And to Jamil, thanks for the running
political commentary.

Chapter 1

Pleasure swept over Ayanna like the warm water that was falling on her naked body. Standing under a waterfall in a secluded cove on a Hawaiian beach, her low moan was swallowed by her lover's mouth, the mouth that had taught her more about love and sensuality than she thought possible. A week ago she wouldn't have believed this kind of abandon was possible, but now she knew for a fact that it could happen. It had happened to her over and over again since their getaway had begun. Ramon had shown her passion beyond belief every day and night, and now he was giving it to her again.

"Ramon." She sighed as his hands tightened on her butt, pulling her closer to his rock-hard manhood. The sigh turned into a sudden gasp as he lifted her so she could straddle him. The powerful muscles of his thighs were braced to hold her as she clung to his broad shoulders. He looked into her eyes, and her already rapid heartbeat seemed to triple. The way he was filling her yearning body was enough to make her faint, but the look in his ebony eyes was drowning her in sensation. Her nipples were so huge and hard she thought they might explode, but Ramon took one in his mouth and sucked hard and fierce so that the only explosion possible was the one they shared as—

"Oh, crap!" Ayanna dropped the handheld shower attachment and groaned. Once again, the boys had used up the hot water before she'd gotten through with her shower. The now ice-cold water had jolted her out of her fantasy. It was her favorite one, too, the closest thing she had to any kind of sex life. *Goodbye, Hawaii; hello, Chicago.* She gritted her teeth resolutely and turned off the water before pulling back the shower curtain and reaching for her towel. As much as she didn't want to spend the money, she was going to have to get a new water heater. Her current one couldn't keep up with the demands of her two adolescent sons.

"When they were little, I practically had to stand over them with a stick to get them to bathe. Now they have to spend an hour apiece in the shower like they're mack daddies or something," she muttered. She wrapped herself in a fluffy pink bath sheet and laughed at her reflection in the mirror. "Well, at least they're clean. And who needs a sex life anyway? I've done without this long. I may as well go for the record."

She patted the excess moisture from her short curly hair and added some leave-in conditioner. With her usual efficiency, she dried her body quickly and put on her favorite scented lotion before getting dressed. It was Saturday morning, and she could have slept in a little longer, but she and the boys were going to a house-warming party that afternoon, and there was breakfast to be cooked and errands to be run before they left.

Ten minutes later she was dressed in jeans and a peach T-shirt and heading to the kitchen with a bag of laundry. Alec, the younger of her sons, appeared in the doorway. He took the laundry from her hands and stopped her from entering the sunny kitchen.

"Don't come in yet, Ma. We're making you a surprise," he said with his endearing smile.

"A surprise? For me? What's the occasion?" She returned the smile, flashing dimples that looked just like Alec's.

Cameron's voice answered. "We just wanted to do something nice for you. Okay, it's all done. You can let her in."

Alec stepped aside and bowed as he gestured Ayanna to the table, which was set for three. "Have a seat, Ma. We made breakfast."

"Aww, you guys are so sweet! What did I do to deserve this?" Ayanna had to blink away tears as she looked at the effort they had put forth. There were cloth napkins with napkin rings and even a bouquet of daisies in the middle of the table. And the food smelled and looked wonderful. "You made me waffles?"

"Yeah, Ma. Waffles and turkey bacon and grits and scrambled eggs. And it's all gonna get cold if you don't sit down and eat," he warned.

Ayanna beamed at the two loves of her life as they bowed their heads to say grace. They had always been sweet, cooperative children, and even now that Alec was fourteen and Cameron was sixteen, they were still good kids. The three of them shared a very strong resemblance, with the same rich brown skin and curly black hair. They all had the same big expressive eyes with long lashes, too; but that was all they shared. Her boys were now young men who towered over her. Ayanna was five-foot-six and slender, and she barely came to their shoulders these days.

Their hearty appetites were to blame for some of their growth. They loved to eat so much that they'd begun to learn how to cook so they could fend for themselves when they went off to college. "These are delicious," Ayanna praised. "And so are the grits and eggs. I can't believe you guys did this all by yourselves."

"I made the waffles and bacon, and Alec did the rest. And we're going to clean up the kitchen, too, as soon as you're done."

She obediently finished off her meal between compliments. "This was the best, guys. And to show you how much I appreciate it, we're going out to dinner after church tomorrow."

"Aww, Ma, you don't have to do that," Cameron protested.

"That's right," Alec added. "We didn't do this to get points or anything."

"That's why we're going to Dave & Buster's tomorrow. Just because you didn't expect a reward," Ayanna told them.

With big smiles on their faces, the brothers gave each other high fives. Dave & Buster's was one of their favorite places to go. They liked the games and excitement as much as the food, and since they didn't go out often, it would be a real treat for the family.

They made good on their promise to clean the kitchen, which they did loudly and cheerfully with Kanye's latest CD blasting as they put things back to rights.

Trying to ignore the loud music, Ayanna put a load of clothes in the washing machine. *Maybe I don't have a love life, but what I do have is wonderful,* she thought. *I have two beautiful boys, a nice home, a good job and a future. Life is good, and sex is probably overrated anyway. Can't miss what you haven't had, now can you?*

A few hours later, their weekly errands were done, and they were on their way to the party.

"So, Ma, did Miss Billie do all the work herself on this house?"

"Pretty much," Ayanna answered. "She designed all the changes and supervised everything, but a crew from

Hunter Construction did the actual work. She got her
hands on a few things, though."

"Billie" was Billie Phillips Wainwright, one of her
bosses at work and a very good friend. She'd been a top
runway model until she quit modeling. Now her career
was in home renovation with her brother-in-law Nick
Hunter. When she married Jason Wainwright he'd surprised her with a big brick mansion, which she had re-
modeled and refurbished. The party was an open house
for all her family and friends to see the end result of her
hard work.

When they pulled up in the big circular driveway of
Billie and Jason's house, there were several cars parked
already. "Alec, will you get the cupcakes, and
Cameron, please take that pan of bread pudding for me?
Thanks, guys." The food was superfluous because all
the women in Billie's family were there and they could
all throw down in the kitchen. But Ayanna's Southern
roots wouldn't let her go anywhere empty-handed, and
her desserts were welcome everywhere because they
were too good to be believed.

The recently wed Wainwrights came out of the side
door of their new home to welcome Ayanna and the
boys. Billie's eyes widened when she saw the packages
being carried by Alec and Cameron. "Yummy! You
shouldn't have, but I'm glad you did. Whatever it is I
know it's good," she said. "Jason, look what Ayanna
brought for the party."

Jason had his arm around Billie's slender waist and
gave her a soft squeeze before greeting Ayanna with a

hug. "I hope it's some German chocolate cake. That last one you made was the bomb. Here, guys, let me take those and you go hang in the back."

Since Jason had inherited some teenage nephews via marriage, Cameron and Alec were more than happy to comply. The backyard with its large patio and the tennis court beckoned, along with the prospect of an afternoon with friends near their age. Billie's big black dog, Sadie, was already in the yard and ran to greet them with her usual happy smile.

Billie held the door open for Jason, and she and Ayanna followed him into the big kitchen with all its new appliances. As Jason put the desserts on the counter, Ayanna grinned at him.

"You're in luck. I made cupcakes. Half are German chocolate and half are red velvet. And there's some pineapple bread pudding, too."

The swinging door between the dining room and the kitchen flew open and a loud voice boomed out. "Did somebody say red velvet? Who said red velvet? Is there seriously some red velvet cake on the premises?"

Ayanna burst into laughter with everyone else except the source of the voice, Billie's older brother, Johnny Phillips.

"Don't play with me. I just came back from the motherland. I've been delayed for hours in every major airport in the world, I may *never* see my other suitcase again and they were talkin' about strip-searching a brother at O'Hare just 'cause they could. So I'm not in the mood to kid around," he said sternly.

The afternoon sun streamed through the windows and glinted off his smooth shaven head. His slightly almond-shaped eyes were intense as his arms were crossed over his bare chest, and he towered over everyone as his expression demanded an immediate answer. Ayanna laughed again.

"Hello, Johnny. It's nice to see you, too," she said pointedly. "Yes, I believe the words *red* and *velvet* were used in the same sentence. Do they have special significance for you?"

Her last words were muffled because Johnny took a couple of steps toward her and gave her a big bear hug that lifted her off the floor. "I'm sorry, Ayanna. I didn't even speak to you, and I'm all over you for your cake. That was just wrong," he said contritely, kissing her on top of her head. "You smell good," he added as he set her down.

"So how was your trip? And how long are you going to be here?" She smiled up at him.

Johnny draped his arm around her shoulders. "I'm not saying another word until I get my fix." He was completely comfortable with his lack of attire, but his younger sister wasn't impressed with his rugged physique.

"Um, I hate to point out the obvious, but why are you in my kitchen half-naked? Where is your shirt?" Billie asked with a frown.

Johnny didn't look embarrassed in the least. He glanced down at his broad chest rippling with muscles and shrugged. "I was on my way to the car to get my stuff when I heard the magic words that made me lose all reason. Are you going to help a brother out or what?" His warm black eyes crinkled in a smile that made Ayanna's knees a little weak, but she ignored the sensation.

"If you put on a shirt, I might let you sample a little somethin'," she teased.

"Sounds like a plan," he agreed and went out the back door, jingling the keys he retrieved from the pocket of his jeans.

She washed her hands at the kitchen sink, and by the time she finished, Johnny was back with a garment bag. "Can I get a taste now? You're not going to make me wait until I go upstairs and put something on, are you?"

Glancing up at him with a grin, she daintily opened the white bakery box and took out a perfect cupcake with a thick, enticing swirl of cream cheese frosting on top.

"Here. Now you've got your fix so you can get dressed and tell me all about your trip to Africa."

"Not yet, woman! Let me savor this before my pop comes in here and we have to fight over it." Johnny had peeled off the cupcake paper and closed his eyes. His strong, even white teeth sank into the pastry, and he devoured it in two bites while moaning like he was in the throes of ecstasy. "Damn, that was good. That tastes like more, 'Yanna. Come on and hook a brother up," he pleaded. "Just one more?"

Ayanna was about to give in to his request when his other sister, Dakota Phillips Hunter, came into the kitchen with her new baby on her shoulder. "Johnny, leave this poor woman alone. What's he trying to get from you, Ayanna?"

By way of answer, Ayanna tipped the box so Dakota could see the cupcakes. "Oh, shoot. Well, you're on your own, girl. Nothing comes between a Phillips man and his need for high-quality sugar in the form of a delicious dessert. The groom's cake at my wedding was red velvet, and he ate the entire thing. I saw him do it. Go for it, brother."

The box had lost all interest for Ayanna. She was much more interested in getting her hands on Dakota's baby girl. "Knock yourself out, Johnny. I want to see this little cupcake right here," she cooed, holding her hands out.

The two women sat down in the dining room so Ayanna could dote on the baby. Johnny helped himself to two more cupcakes before joining them. "Ayanna, you're gorgeous, and you can cook. If I was a marrying man, I'd be chasing you down," he said sincerely.

Ayanna laughed softly and looked at little Bethany Anne Hunter, who was gurgling softly in her arms. "Sweetie pie, your uncle is nice, but he's crazy."

Johnny polished off the third cake with a deep sigh of enjoyment and licked a bit of frosting off his finger. "I might be crazy, but I know a good woman when I see one," he said with a wink.

The blush only showed on her cheeks, but Ayanna could feel it from the bottom of her feet all the way to the top of her head as she pretended that she wasn't listening to his joking. She cuddled Bethany to her shoulder and inhaled her sweet baby scent before stealing a look in Johnny's direction. Luckily, he was talking to Dakota, and she got a good look at his long, muscular frame and sexy rear end. Her face filled with heat again as he turned just in time to see her staring at him, and he winked at her again; but this time it was slow and sexy. She knew she looked like a critter caught in the high beams of a semi, but she couldn't look away to save herself.

She really didn't have a choice in the matter because someone came into the room to join them.

"Johnny, sweetheart, what is taking you so long? I've been waiting for you," a feminine voice purred.

Ayanna felt a weird sensation creep over her, but it wasn't the same pleasurable feeling she'd enjoyed earlier. This was dangerously close to jealousy, something she hadn't experienced in years. And she hadn't missed it one bit, either.

Chapter 2

Ayanna had to put on her best game face and act as though nothing were amiss, when in reality, she was a little unnerved to hear the dulcet tones of Dr. Davina Wainwright. She was Jason's sister, and she never let anyone forget that she was the most beautiful woman in the room as well as one of the top cosmetic surgeons on the East Coast. She was also one of the snottiest people Ayanna had ever met in her life. The only one who could top her was Cloris, the other Wainwright sister. She, too, was a plastic surgeon.

Both the sisters were tall and thin and quite pretty in a heavily painted sort of way. Since Billie had married into their family they had toned down a little bit of the diva behavior because they were never the prettiest anything when the Phillips sisters were in the room. They had refused Billie's invitation to be her brides- maids, but once they found out that Billie's wedding was featured in every fashion publication in this country as well as the UK and France, they realized what a huge mistake they'd made in being rude and changed their tune.

When they saw all of Billie's A-list celebrity friends at the wedding and reception, they had done as Jason predicted and tried to join Billie at the hip. Luckily, Billie saw right through them like they were glass. Both of them lived in New York, but lately they'd spent a lot of weekends in Chicago. Ayanna had once sug- gested that they were trying to make amends, and Billie had just rolled her eyes.

"That's sweet, Ayanna, but their motives have nothing to do with being sisterly. It's all about meeting potential celebrity clients and maybe a man or two. Nip and Tuck don't fool me a bit," Billie had said with a sniff.

Ayanna wasn't about to let the presence of one of the snotty sisters ruin her day. She enjoyed being around Billie and Dakota too much to allow the woman to get on her nerves. She toured the house with Billie, who was as excited as a kid on Christmas morning to show off her dream house.

"The floors are bamboo, because it's a sustainable resource. And all the paint is environmentally friendly, too," she said as they looked in the second floor rooms. Billie put her arm around Ayanna's shoulders and gave her a sisterly hug. "I don't know why I'm telling you this. You were with me when I picked out a lot of this stuff. I'm just house-proud right now," she admitted.

"And you should be," Ayanna said. "This place is magnificent. One day I'm going to have a bigger place. I love my house, but the walls are going to close in on us in a little while. The boys are getting so big!"

"These walls are going to close in soon, to hear Jason tell it. He's decided he wants a bunch of kids and as soon as possible," she murmured with a blush.

"And somehow I think you're going to indulge him in this wish, aren't you?" Ayanna stopped peeking into the bedrooms and ceased walking so abruptly that Billie bumped into her. "You're pregnant already, aren't you?"

By way of answer, Billie just showed all her perfect teeth in a big grin. "That question will be answered this afternoon. But if you can keep a secret for a couple of hours, the answer is *yes*. Jason was determined I get pregnant on our honeymoon, but it took a little longer than that. But in about six months, there's going to be another baby around here."

Ayanna's face lit up. "First Toni and Zane with little Brandon, then Dakota and Nick with little Bethany and now you and Jason are getting ready to add to the mix. Y'all don't mess around when it comes to popping out those babies. Do any of you folks wait a year before reproducing?" she teased.

She was referring to Zane Beauchamp and his wife Toni. Zane owned the paper where Dakota worked.

Dakota and Toni were very close and their babies were a few months apart in age.

Billie laughed. "It was almost a year for me and Jason. Of the three couples, we showed the most restraint," she said airily.

"Y'all are gonna be *in* restraints when junior keeps you up all night." Johnny emerged from one of the guest rooms, this time fully dressed and looking good. "I don't know how people put up with all that racket. Ayanna, you have two boys, how did you handle the late-night feedings, the colic, walking them all night, potty training and all the other fun things nobody tells you about being a parent?"

He ducked when Billie aimed a punch at his shoulder. "Hey, I'm just trying to get somebody to talk sense into you people. There'll be babies all over this house in a few years if you don't cool your jets. Tell her about it, Ayanna."

Her face had changed into a rigid mask bearing a stiff and very phony smile. "I can't help you there. I didn't go through all of that with my boys. I adopted Alec when he was four and Cameron was six, so I got to miss all the fun of carrying a baby I loved from inception to delivery. I'm, um, going to go see what they're up to. See you later," she added hurriedly as she dashed down the stairs.

Johnny looked helplessly at Billie, who was staring at him with great exasperation. "You have a big mouth, you know that?" she said.

"How was I supposed to know I was saying something stupid? You never know when you've said something stupid until it's out there and you've made a daggone fool out of yourself," he said gruffly. "You could have given me a heads-up. You know I like her, and this is the first time we've had a chance to get together."

Billie didn't have time to ponder this revelation because Johnny was still talking. "Besides, those kids look just like her. How come they look like triplets if they're not hers?"

Billie sighed and put her hand on her brother's arm. "Because they're related by blood. Those boys are her sister's children. She died when the boys were quite young, and Ayanna was their guardian. She adopted them and has done her best to raise them to be the delightful young men they are today." Billie looked reflective for a moment. "She's sacrificed a lot for Alec and Cameron, although she doesn't consider it to be any kind of burden. They're her whole life, and she loves them devotedly.

"Now what's this about you liking Ayanna?" she asked with a frown. "Your track record with the ladies isn't one I want to wish upon my best friend. If you want to play, stay away from my girl. She's isn't your normal disposable party favor, so don't even think about it."

The warm clasp on his arm was replaced by a sharp pinch. He jerked away from her looking stunned. "That was just wrong, Billie. In the first place, you make me sound like some ol' cheap playa, and in the second place, I think you left a mark, you wildcat. Does Jason know about this side of you?"

"I don't think you're cheap," she said earnestly. "I think you're a very high-priced playa, top-shelf, in fact." She turned to run down the stairs and looked at him over her shoulder. "And Jason knows all about my wild side, and he loves it. He encourages it," she added, wiggling her hips as Johnny covered his ears and made a horrible face.

"Oversharing, little sister. That's called oversharing."

Ayanna felt like a nitwit for her reaction to Johnny's innocent remarks. After she reached the first floor, she got a glimpse of Davina regaling Toni and Zane Beauchamp with a story about her illustrious medical practice, and Ayanna quickly slipped out of the French doors that led to the big terrazzo patio. It was a soothing place with comfortable chairs and big potted plants surrounded by a low brick wall. Taking a deep breath, she watched her boys playing a noisy game of basketball with Nick's nephews. Sadie was also playing, running back and forth and barking with gusto.

Why did I act like that? It's not the first time the subject has come up, she thought. *So why did I act like I was running from the law or something?*

Just then she felt two strong hands on her shoulders. Johnny turned her around to face him. "I didn't mean to say anything out of line, Ayanna. Are we still friends?"

She looked up at his handsome face, which was completely serious for the first time she could remember. Johnny was always laughing and making jokes, so this was quite a change. "We're fine. You didn't know my boys are adopted, and there's no real reason that you should've known. But it's not like it's a secret," she told him.

He nodded and continued to look at her like he was trying to memorize her face. "I just realized that I don't know very much about you," he said thoughtfully.

Ayanna was looking at him with the same kind of intensity. "No, I guess you don't. I met you at Billie's wedding, and I've seen you a few times since then. It's not like you live here in Chicago or anything."

Johnny didn't seem to be listening to her. His big palms were making circles on her shoulders, and he showed no interest in removing his hands from her body. But he was paying attention, as his next words demonstrated. "Well, I think we should start remedying that. I'm moving here, and I think getting to know you better is going to be a priority."

"You're moving here? Permanently?" Ayanna sounded slightly breathless.

"Yes, I am. Didn't Billie tell you? Let's get something to eat and talk about it some more."

"Is food all you think about?"

"Pretty much. Food and sex. What else is there, besides football?" Johnny's face resumed its normal, humorous expression as he smiled down at her.

Ayanna's eyes widened. "You need Jesus, Johnny Phillips. You need help."

"So are you gonna help a brother out or what?" His hands flew off her shoulders as he heard Davina's voice float out through the French doors. "Billie, where's that brother of yours? He just disappeared."

"Help me get away from that succubus," Johnny said urgently. "She's been on me like a duck on a june bug, and I'm trying not to hurt her feelings. Come on. Let's go in the side door."

"Johnny, you're crazy!" Ayanna's dimples wreathed her smile as she allowed him to hustle her away from the sound of Davina's voice.

"No, I'm not. I need help, just like you said. Help me stay away from the man-eater and I'll give you anything you want."

A warm pleasant feeling settled over her at his teasing words. "Don't make promises you can't keep. You have no idea what I might want," she warned.

They had reached the door that led to the kitchen. He squeezed her hand, which he'd taken when he led her off the patio. "That's true, I don't. But whatever it is, I'll give it to you gladly. Count on that," he replied with his devastating grin.

They went into the big kitchen, and he stared at the table loaded with all kinds of good things to eat.

"Dang, that looks good. Fix me a plate, and we'll get started on your list." Johnny went to the sink and washed his hands while Ayanna stared at his beautiful butt and his long legs that were slightly bowed.

"I'll fix you a plate, but what list are you talking about?"

He turned around, wiping his hands on a dish towel. "Your desires, Ayanna. I told you I'd give you anything you want."

She couldn't move for a moment, and then she laughed at his foolishness. "Move out of the way so I can wash my hands. Your blood sugar must be low."

Chapter 3

After the party ended and everyone went home, Johnny was still thinking about Ayanna. He'd insisted on following her home to make sure she got there safely, even though it was kind of superfluous seeing as how it was barely dark and she had Alec and Cameron for protection. He did it anyway and pulled up in the driveway behind them. He watched until they were all in the house safely, and then he punched in her number on his cell phone.

"I told you I was going to call you," he'd reminded her. She had laughed, the tinkling little giggle that reminded him of spring rain.

"Yes, but I didn't think you'd be calling from the driveway. You want to come in and have a cup of coffee?"

He had done so at once because it gave him a chance to see her again, even for a little while. He had admired her house and got to observe her easy relationship with the boys up close. Actually, he'd spent more time talking with Alec and Cameron than he had with Ayanna, but it was cool because he liked them. She had raised some fine young men. She'd finally called the evening to a halt because they had to get up early for church the next day. He would see her there since she and Billie and Dakota attended the same church, and he always went with them when he was in town.

Now Johnny was in the media room of Billie's house, stretched out on one of the big leather sofas. The plasma TV was on ESPN, but he wasn't watching it. He was thinking about Ayanna's smile. She'd made an impression on him the first moment he'd seen her at Billie's wedding. He'd gotten into Chicago the morning of the ceremony, and he'd missed all the festivities leading up to it, so he hadn't seen the bridesmaids until they were walking down the aisle. Her huge black eyes, the big dimples and her perfect golden brown complexion were all adorable, but he'd thought she was about nineteen or twenty, way too young for him.

After the ceremony he'd found out that Alec and Cameron, who'd played the violin and piano during the ceremony, were her sons. This made him think she was married. By the time he realized she was single, the reception was almost over and he'd hooked up with some tall leggy woman who was into a good time for one night only, which was his style. He remembered, though, watching Ayanna dance the night away with what seemed like every man there. She could dance her butt off, he recalled, in a sexy and alluring but not sleazy way. She was graceful and moved like she'd been doing it all her life.

Billie entered the room and interrupted his thoughts. "Who won the game?"

"Huh?" He turned to look at her. "Who won what?"

She pushed his feet aside and sat down on the end of the couch. "Were you asleep? I asked who won. Aren't you watching the scores?" she asked as she pointed to the TV.

"No, I was thinking about Ayanna. She's beautiful, isn't she?"

Billie tilted her head as she looked him over. "If you were any other man on the planet, I'd say you were smitten, but we know that's not true, don't we?"

"You don't know anything, little sister. Where did she learn how to dance like that?"

"She used to be on a dance squad when she was in high school, I think, and she took dance when she was little. She teaches a dance class at a community center near her house. That girl can get down like a pro," she said. "Wait, I have a DVD from the hospital benefit. Todd asked her to be his partner in this ballroom dance thing. Hold on, let me get it." Todd Wainwright, Jason's younger brother, had missed the party because he was at work.

She rose gracefully and went to the wall where the DVDs were stored. "Let's see…" she murmured. "Oh, here it is. I'll put it in for you."

Jason appeared in the doorway as she slipped the disc into the player. "Baby, isn't it time for you to go to bed? You did a lot today, and I don't want you to tire yourself out," he said.

Billie went to him and nuzzled the base of his throat as he wrapped her in his arms. "I was just getting ready to come upstairs. I'm a little tired, but not because I did too much. You did everything for me, as usual."

Johnny sat up and waved the couple off. "Take your lovey-dovey newlywed expectant-parent selves out of here before I get sick from watching you," he said.

"Aw, man, don't hate, participate," Jason drawled. "This is what you get when you turn in your playa card and start being a real man." He stopped talking and kissed Billie deeply.

"I'm blind, I'm blind," Johnny moaned. "Stop doing that, man, that's my baby sister."

Billie and Jason shouted with laughter. "I might be your sister, but I'm his wife. This is what married life is like."

"Yeah, well I may never know. Good *night. Please,* good night, sleep well, etcetera. By the way, speaking of sisters, where is yours?" He pointed at Jason as he spoke.

"She hooked up with some quarterback or whatever. We might not see her until tomorrow," Jason answered. "See ya."

Johnny pumped his fist in the air as the couple left. "Thank you! Now I can have some peace." He pushed play on the DVD player and was immediately transfixed by what he saw on the high definition screen. "Oh damn, I could be in serious trouble," he murmured as he watched Ayanna come into view. "But it's just the kind of trouble I like."

Ayanna was thinking about the events of the day as she got ready for bed. The party was wonderful, just like any gathering with Billie's family. They had to be the sweetest people she'd ever met. Dakota's in-laws and Billie and Dakota's parents were just delightful. And what could you say about Johnny Phillips? He was every woman's dream—tall, intelligent, funny and kind and his looks were off the chart. Too bad he was way out of her league. Men like Johnny ended up with women like his sisters: Billie, the former supermodel who was now making her mark in the construction business, and Dakota, the Pulitzer prize-winning author who'd also won an Oscar for screenwriting. Yes, with sisters like that, he'd look for a doctor, a CEO or even a lawyer, since that was his profession. Standards had been set pretty high in the Phillips family.

She was in her bedroom, taking a last look in the mirror before getting in the shower. A pleasant face looked back at her. Her skin was good; her hair was passable, although it wasn't long and cascading like the Phillips women. *I guess I could get a fifteen-hundred-dollar weave like Davina,* she thought. She made a face at her reflection. *No need to take a swallow of haterade. You are what you are.*

She took off the cute celery-green cotton sweater

she'd worn with a pair of light-colored jeans and a pair of stylish little yellow flats from Payless. She laughed as she took off the shoes to put them in the closet. She couldn't see Johnny Phillips with a woman who scouted for clothes on clearance at Target and shoes from the Payless buy one, get one sales. She wasn't a high-powered executive or someone of national prominence. She was a single mother with an office job who had to pinch pennies hard to make sure her sons were well-fed, nicely clothed, safe and secure. And that her bills were paid on time. She didn't drive a luxury car, unless a five-year-old PT Cruiser was in that category. Her house was sparkling clean and charming, but almost everything had been done by her two hands, assisted by the boys. Nope, she was not his glass of champagne, not by a long shot.

She finished undressing and took a long shower. It was the only way she could be sure to get some hot water because the boys would monopolize it the next morning before church. Sighing as the sweet scent of her bath gel filled her nostrils, she thought again about how much fun she'd had with Johnny. She loved his irreverent humor and outrageous flirting; she was so busy being a mom she'd forgotten how much fun it could be. Ayanna could be shy with people she didn't know, but her acquaintance with Johnny and his family made him feel safe and familiar. For a brief moment she wished with all her heart that she was more than what she was. She wished she was the kind of woman who could attract a man like Johnny for real.

* * *

Ayanna couldn't wait to get to church the next morning to pray for forgiveness. The dreams she'd had the night before were so vivid and explicit that she'd awakened sweaty, trembling and moist in places that should have been bone dry. And "Ramon" was not the star attraction that night. He'd been replaced by someone taller, broader of shoulder and chocolate brown with a clean shaven head. She didn't need an advanced degree in psychology to know what that was about. She kicked the covers off and glanced at the clock on the bedside table. It was 5:00 a.m. She sat up groggily and tossed aside the wrinkled bedclothes. She needed another shower to wash away all traces of her drastically misplaced erotic desires.

She scrubbed herself from head to toe, using her nylon bath puff like a weapon. When she washed her small, firm breasts and the sensitive area between her legs, she was dismayed to find them tender and responsive to her touch, as though the wild sex of her dream was real. To shake off all vestiges of her nocturnal fantasies, she lowered the temperature of the shower until it was quite cool. She had to stifle a scream, but she ran the cold water over her body resolutely and thoroughly. If anyone knew what she'd been thinking, she'd die of shame.

Okay, that's a little dramatic, she admitted as she toweled herself dry. But the things they had done to each other in that dream were so vivid and so wild! *I've got to leave those romance novels alone.* No more

Brenda Jackson, Maureen Smith or Altonya Washington for her. And definitely no more Adrianne Byrd! The books she read were well-written, delightfully sensual and they'd been her obsession ever since she discovered African-American romance. She had so many of the books that she had to catalog them.

The newest ones were in her to-be-read pile next to the bed. Her favorites took a place of honor in her bedroom bookcase. The older books were in boxes under her bed, each box labeled with a sheet that told the name and author of each book. She sighed heavily as she made her bed, still wrapped in her towel. It was pathetic enough that her sex life was confined to reading the delicious love scenes the authors so generously provided her in their fascinating books, but when her loneliness—and yes, her unfulfilled desires—made her include a real live man in her dreams, well, it was time for a change.

I'm the one who needs help, she thought. *Maybe there's some kind of herbal thing I can get at the health food store to cool my jets.* She had to laugh out loud at that thought. It wasn't that serious. She just needed to exercise more. That would work out those urges quite nicely. She could teach another dance class; it would give the boys more time at the rec center, which they would enjoy. Problem solved. No more crazy dreams about having wild sex in the middle of a bed with red satin sheets with a chocolate hunk of man for her. She would exercise that man right out of her thighs, that's what she would do.

She looked around, realized that she'd made the bed, rearranged her dresser and organized her closet. And she still had over thirty minutes before the boys' alarm would go off. Okay, she'd put on her underwear and a robe and go make some cinnamon rolls for a surprise. Keeping busy was the answer. If she just kept busy and kept her mind focused on productive things, she had no doubt that her current state of constant longing would dissipate. It was a good plan that only took a few hours to blow up in her face.

Chapter 4

Johnny slept a lot better than Ayanna, and the dreams he had about being with her weren't a cause for angst. On the contrary, he was looking forward to seeing her that morning. He'd watched the DVD of her dancing three times before he went to bed, after making a point of taking it out of the player and taking it to the guest room with him. He had every intention of keeping it, and Billie could just get over it until he could copy it. *If* he copied it. For some reason, he didn't really want anyone else looking at it. The way Ayanna looked was amazing, but the way she was dancing was too sexy to be believed.

He was still in bed, wearing the sheet that was covering him and nothing else. He smiled lazily as he recalled with total clarity every act of consensual loving he'd shared with Ayanna during the night. It was the costume she'd worn in the DVD that had done it. It was some kind of gold getup with those sparkly things on it. It had a top part with one shoulder strap and a skirt thing that bared her navel and was split on the side to show off her long, shapely legs. Ayanna might be slender, but every inch of her was bangin' as his early-morning tent pole testified.

He chuckled as he enjoyed the sensation of his erection. Some men got bothered by the early-morning wake-up call by their nether regions, but Johnny liked it. It let him know that he was still in business, and after the night of fantasies he'd had courtesy of the captivating Ayanna, he couldn't blame his body for reacting. The way she had worked her body around that stage was so blazing hot it had seared his eyeballs. She moved like she didn't have any bones in her hips, especially when she was doing the Latin dances. She had such control of her beautiful body that all he could think was what she would feel like in his arms.

The only hitch was Todd Wainwright. Were they involved or something? Todd hadn't made it to the open house because he was head of the trauma unit at John Stroger Hospital, and he'd been on call yesterday. They seemed to move as one person on the DVD, and the way he touched her and looked into her eyes during the dance was more intimate than Johnny liked. Was it part of the show, or was there something going on? He'd already made two wrong assumptions about

Ayanna that had put him off the trail, and he wasn't
going to make a third. First he assumed she was too
young, and then he assumed she had a husband because
she had two sons. "Yeah, well, they say assumptions
are the mothers of all screwups. I'm getting to the
bottom of this ASAP," he said aloud.

He tossed back the covers and got out of the bed,
stretching as he did so. First a long hot shower, then a
little grooming of his goatee and a shave of his cheeks.
Then he'd get dressed for church before going downstairs to grill his sister about her brother-in-law's inten-
tions toward the delightful Ayanna. This time he was
going to get it right.

Johnny came into the kitchen to find Billie and his
mother at the table. He kissed them both, and after ex-
changing greetings, he got right down to business.
"Billie, what's the deal with Todd and Ayanna? Are
they kickin' it or what?"

Lee Phillips looked at her oldest child with equal parts
amusement and amazement. "You sound rather territorial,
dear. What's going on? Are you interested in Ayanna?"

Johnny didn't hesitate. "Yeah, I sure am. Why
shouldn't I be interested? She's smart, she's a great
mother, her boys are well-mannered, well-behaved and
intelligent and she's gorgeous. Why are you asking if
I'm interested? Don't you like her? You think there's
something wrong with her?" He had a very defined
scowl on his face, which neither woman had ever seen
on behalf of a woman.

Lee and Billie exchanged glances before bursting into laughter.

"I think he's serious, Mama," Billie said. "I'm going to finish cooking breakfast before Daddy comes down here growling like a bear."

"Come sit down, dear." Lee invited him. "Have some coffee."

"I'm not sitting down until you tell me why you don't like Ayanna," he said defensively. "She's a lovely woman. What's not to like about her?"

"Ooh, you're really going off the deep end, aren't you?" Lee's eyes twinkled with affection for her son. "Now sit your lanky butt down, and let me drop some knowledge on you."

Johnny sat down at the pub table in the spacious kitchen and crossed his arms on the table. Lee took a sip of coffee before speaking.

"Ayanna Porter is an outstanding young woman, and your father and I adore her. But she's not like those gangly airheads you normally spend two or three weeks wining, dining, bedding and forgetting. She's not for you, son. All you want is a good time, and she's not a good time gal. So unless you're willing to go the distance, you need to go away." Her words were kind but firm.

"Don't hold back, Mama. How do you really feel about it?" he said dryly.

Billie's giggles could be heard as she took a tray of maple crisped turkey bacon out of the oven. "I guess she told you, big brother. But she's right. I told you,

Ayanna ain't anybody's play toy. If you're looking for a playmate, I think I heard Davina in the shower. She got in late, but she should be rarin' to go."

"Well, thanks for the gratifying assessment of my personality," Johnny said curtly. "I think I'll just meet you at church," he added.

"Oh, don't get mad. I made stuffed French toast," Billie wheedled. "It's Ayanna's recipe. We're not trying to say that you're a hound, but you haven't had any long, sustaining relationships. Unless that's what you're looking for, Ayanna's not the one for you. She deserves someone who's going to love her unconditionally and permanently and that hasn't been your pattern, you have to admit."

Jason came into the room and kissed his wife before going to his mother-in-law and giving her a good morning kiss on the cheek. "I heard you all when I was coming through the dining room. Ease up off Johnny. I was a coast-to-coast hound before I met Billie. When a man meets the right woman, he becomes the right man for her. Am I right, baby?" he asked, looking at Billie.

"Yes, you are," she answered. "Johnny, there may be hope for you yet."

Johnny didn't respond to her encouraging words. "Jason, maybe I can get a straight answer from you. Are Todd and Ayanna involved?"

Jason looked surprised. "No, not at all. They're friends and occasional dance partners, but Todd is too wrapped up in his work to get into a relationship. If he was, I'd know because his mouth runs like water. They're totally friends," he assured Johnny.

Johnny's face relaxed into its normal smile. "That's good to know."

The outside door opened, and Johnny's father, Boyd, walked in with Sadie, who was glad to see everyone. "What's good to know? Where's my breakfast? My grand-dog and I are ready to eat."

Johnny was fondling Sadie's ears and didn't answer. Lee was more than happy to fill in the details, though.

"Your son was finding out whether or not the adorable Ayanna Porter was involved. He's happy that's she's available," she said archly.

Boyd shrugged his broad shoulders as he went to inspect the spread Billie was preparing. "I'm glad to know that, too. It's about time you settled down, son."

Everyone waited for Johnny's usual declaration that he was going to stay single forever, but it wasn't forthcoming. "You could be right, Pop," was all he said. "You want me to set the table, little sister?"

Lee and Billie were shocked by his laconic response, but Boyd and Jason acted as though nothing was amiss. Mother and daughter exchanged a look that said they'd be talking about this at great length once they were alone.

Ayanna's peace was invaded once again when she saw Johnny at church. She had been enveloped in the serenity that always surrounded her every Sunday, when she got a tap on the shoulder. Turning around to find the source of the tap, she saw Johnny looking even better than usual in a fabulous gray suit. His shirt was pale blue and his silk tie had a rep pattern in shades of blue and gray and to make matters worse, he smelled terrific. He was smiling at her, too, which made her heart give a few extra beats. Great, fine, swell. Here she had just prayed the man out of her mind and here he was in the flesh, temptation personified. She mustered a smile and a greeting.

"I didn't see you earlier. Where were you sitting?" she asked politely.

"We were sitting about two rows behind you. I saw you," he said with that darned sexy smile. "You look good from the back, but even better from the front."

Ayanna felt a bit of heat from his words. She always liked getting dressed up for church, and she'd worn a pink linen Ralph Lauren suit she'd gotten from the consignment shop. It was brand new, too; the tags were still on it. It was her favorite spring outfit, and hearing his compliment was nice but unsettling considering the blazing hot dream she was trying to delete from her mental hard drive.

He took her arm like they'd been walking together for years, and before she knew it, they were outside the church with his family. She greeted everyone and looked around for Alec and Cameron. The sooner they got out of there, the better it would be for her peace of mind.

Cameron came out of nowhere, and she breathed a sigh of relief. "Where's your brother?" she asked, after he exchanged polite greetings with everyone.

"He's headed to the car, I think. He said he was starving." Cameron grinned.

"Well, why don't you all come on over to the house? We've got tons of leftovers, so we thought we'd just have a second-day party," Billie said.

"Thanks, but I told the boys I'd take them to Dave & Buster's," Ayanna said.

"One of my favorite restaurants," Johnny said. "Mind if I tag along?"

"No, that would be great," Cameron assured him. "I wanted to ask you some more questions about your foundation, if that's okay, Mr. Phillips."

Ayanna looked down at the peep toes of her Payless wedge-heeled beige sandals. Why did her children have to have such good manners? She looked up to see Johnny pointing at his father.

"That's Mr. Phillips over there. Just call me John," he said. "Why don't we go in my car?"

Ayanna finally found her voice and said something about changing clothes. That's how they wound up in a mini-caravan, with Johnny following her to the small brick home she shared with the boys. Cameron and Alec rode with Johnny, and she led the way, giving herself a pep talk as she drove.

"Quit being a drama queen. It's just an afternoon with the boys and Johnny. It's not like it's a date. He has no idea that you have a dirty little mind, and there's no reason for him to find out. Just chill, and try to act like a grown woman instead of a schoolgirl," she mumbled.

She pulled into the driveway and was already at the back door when Johnny and the boys arrived. Alec and Cameron bounded out of the SUV with Johnny following at a more sedate pace.

"Mom, we got an idea on the way over here. Guess what John's favorite meal is?" Cameron asked.

"I couldn't possibly. What is it?" she asked faintly.

"Lasagna! We told him what a good cook you are and how good your lasagna is, and I know there's some in the freezer, so why don't we all have dinner here?"

Alec joined in the plea, double-teaming her. "Yeah, Ma, that would be fun. Can we stay here, please?"

Ayanna looked at their pleading faces helplessly. They were so hard to resist when they asked for something—and they asked for so little. She bought some time by opening the back door and entering the kitchen. She put her purse and keys on the table and turned to face the three of them. "But this was supposed to be a treat for you guys," she said. "I'm sure Johnny would rather go to the restaurant than eat here. Besides, I don't have any Italian bread and, umm…" She vainly tried to think of other reasons why this was a bad idea.

"I can't think of anything I'd like more than eating here with you and the guys. And if you need anything from the store, we'd be happy to go get it for you. We'll clean up afterward, too. And," Johnny added persuasively, "I'll take you all out to Dave & Buster's later in the week or on the weekend or whenever you like. How's that for a deal?"

Ayanna looked at the three pairs of eyes that were

all beseeching her to agree, and she caved. "Fine. I'll get the lasagna out while you guys change clothes, and then you can go pick up a few things for me. And that kitchen had better be spotless," she said playfully.

"Cool!" Alec and Cameron slapped each other five while Johnny gave her a satisfied smile. She wondered what she had just gotten herself into.

Chapter 5

Dinner was actually a lot more fun than Ayanna
expected. After the boys went to change out of their
church clothes, Johnny surprised her by going out to
his SUV and coming back in the house with a garment
bag. He explained that he was in the process of moving.

"I just got in yesterday morning, and most of my
things are still in the car. I'm going to stay at Nick's
old apartment until I get a house. So if you don't mind,
I'm going to get into something more casual so I don't
get sauce on my good suit."

"Of course you can," Ayanna said. "Come on, I'll
take you to the spare room, and you can change there."

She led him down the hall to a small room that she
had set up as a place where the boys could do their

homework and she could work from home. It had a chaise lounge, a comfortable chair and a computer desk. Like all the rooms in her house, it was neat as a pin as well as attractive. Warm cocoa walls, bamboo blinds and several colorful prints made it warm and welcoming. There were green plants hanging in the two windows and an African-inspired print rug on the hardwood floor.

"Here you go. You can hang your garment bag on the back of the door or in the closet," she said, ignoring the warmth that invaded her as he stood close to her body. He took her hand and gave her a look that could have melted a glacier.

"Thanks, Ayanna. I really appreciate you doing this. I don't want to put you to any trouble, but I don't get home-cooked food for months at a time, so I really look forward to it when I can get some," he told her.

The feel of his big hand wrapped around hers was intoxicating, but she forced herself to speak in a normal voice and act casual. "It's no bother at all, don't be silly. I'm going to make a list while you change."

Johnny's compelling eyes continued to lock with hers. "Is this your grocery list or the list of the desires I'm going to fulfill?"

"Groceries! I'll need my computer to list everything I want from you," she said without thinking. She was glad he took it as a joke, and the sound of his laughter followed her down the hall. Her hands were trembling while she jotted down a few things to round out their meal. She went to the refrigerator and poured a big glass of ice-cold water, which she drank rapidly in an effort to cool off the fire that he ignited in her. *It's just dinner. Just one dinner, and then things will be back to normal. Try to act like you got some sense,* she chided herself.

In a few minutes Alec, Cameron and Johnny presented themselves in jeans and T-shirts and announced that they were ready to do her bidding.

"Here you go. They boys can tell you where the store is, and they know what brands I like. I think they do, don't they?" She glanced at her sons, who looked amused.

"Of course we do, Ma. Give us some credit," Cameron said. "We know everything you like."

Johnny looked mischievous and said, "Good, you can give me some pointers on how to get on her good side." They went out the door like they'd been hanging out for years, and Ayanna stared after them until she reminded herself that she had work to do.

She went to the side-by-side refrigerator and pulled open the freezer door. Ayanna liked to power cook, as she called it. If she made spaghetti or chili or macaroni and cheese, things her sons really liked, she would double or triple the recipe so that there were always two or three casseroles in the freezer to be popped in the oven at a moment's notice. She took out the lasagna and put it on a cookie sheet before sliding it into the oven. She would make garlic bread and stuff some mushrooms with pesto to round out the meal along with a big green salad.

By the time the guys came back from the store, she had changed into some nice fitting jeans and a violet scoop-necked T-shirt that showed off her figure without being too provocative. She was also wearing lavender flip-flops, and her toenails were polished in a pretty shade of pink. "Thank you, gentlemen. Now if you go play some ball or watch the game or something, dinner will be ready in about forty-five minutes."

Alec stayed to set the dining room table for her while she made the garlic bread and the stuffed mush-rooms. The salad took no time, since she used a pre-bagged mixture of romaine lettuce.

"I can do that for you, Ma," Alec offered.

"Thanks, sweetie. You're too good to me," she said.

"Aww, Ma, cut it out. I'm supposed to be good to you because you're so sweet and nice and you do everything for us. We're lucky to have you for a mother," he said.

Her eyes filled with tears, and she started to hug him but he held up the oversized salad forks like a cross. "No mushy stuff, Ma! Step away, or I'll put something weird in the salad."

"Like what?" Ayanna smiled. Like typical adoles-cents, both Alec and Cameron had moments when the "mushy stuff" was just too much for them to handle.

"Grub worms, locusts, lizards, stuff like that. John said people in Africa eat them. They're a delicacy in some places."

"Ewwww! My palate isn't that sophisticated, thank you."

"John is a really cool guy, isn't he? He's really smart,

and he's done a lot of traveling. He's the kind of guy you should date," he added innocently.

"Okay, thanks for your help. Tell Cameron and Johnny to wash up and dinner will be on the table in about fifteen minutes," she said hurriedly. When he left the room, she leaned against the counter and sighed deeply. What next?

Ayanna was used to getting compliments on her cooking, but Johnny looked and acted as though he'd been transported to some idyllic land when he tasted her meal. He praised the garlic bread and the mushrooms, but he declared his love for the main course.

"This is the most magnificent meal I've had in a long time. I don't know how to thank you for allowing me to disrupt your family time," he said.

"Oh, that's easy. You guys are cleaning up the kitchen, remember?"

Alec and Cameron were already clearing the table and bringing in dessert, which was raspberry sorbet and some of her homemade brownies, which had been known to make people swoon when they tasted them. Johnny was in that category. His eyes lit up when he saw them, and when he swallowed his first bite, he closed his eyes in bliss.

"Alec, Cameron, I know we don't know each other too well, but once I marry your mother, we're going to be good friends. Sound okay to you?"

Suddenly the tension that had been building in Ayanna dissipated, and she started laughing. This was the Johnny she'd been getting to know, and this was his usual exaggerated sense of humor. So what if he'd visited her dreams? Stuff happened, and you got over it. "Johnny, you really do need Jesus," she said.

"Ma, why do you call him Johnny? He told us to call him John," Cameron pointed out.

"I can help you with that. My dad named us all after singers. I was named after Johnny Hartman, this amazing jazz singer. So Johnny is my given name, but I usually tell people to call me John because it just sounds more adult, more businesslike," he admitted.

Alec, ever-curious, had to ask another question. "So why don't you tell Ma to call you John?"

Johnny looked directly into Ayanna's eyes. "Because I like the way she says my name."

"You did an excellent job on the kitchen," Ayanna said. Dinner was over, and the promise to clean up was fulfilled. Alec and Cameron were at a friend's house, and it was just Ayanna and Johnny, sitting on the sofa listening to music and talking.

"You did a superlative job on everything else," Johnny said. "You're an amazing woman, Ayanna. Besides being beautiful and a perfect mother, you cook like a Cordon Bleu graduate, and you dance like a professional. How did you learn to dance like that?"

"Like what? Oh no, did Billie show you that DVD?" She covered her face and groaned.

Johnny pulled her hands away from her face. "Don't

go getting all shy with me. You could be headlining in Vegas or Miami with those moves."

"I didn't think she was going to show it to anyone."

"She won't be showing it to anyone else. I stole it from her just so I could keep it to myself," he said.

"Are you kidding me? You actually took it? Why?"

"Because it turned me on." He leaned toward her. "You were too hot for anyone else to see. You kept me up all night thinking about the way you moved, the way you looked. You were blazin' hot, Ayanna. Do you still have that little outfit you wore?"

"That's for me to know and you to find out, if you can," she said sassily.

"Don't dare me," Johnny warned. "I've been known to play dirty to get what I want."

"Don't threaten me," she said. "I'm the one with the brownies, remember?"

Johnny held his hands up in supplication. "You win."

Ayanna turned her head toward the stereo and then looked back at Johnny. "What is that playing? It's beautiful."

"That is John Coltrane. The singer is Johnny Hartman. He's the only vocalist Coltrane ever recorded with. That's the man I was named for. You like him?"

"I love his voice. It's like velvet."

"You can keep that one. I just happened to have it in the car stereo, and I thought you might like it."

"You're very thoughtful. Would you like some coffee?"

"Only if I can have another brownie."

"It's yours. Come with me."

Soon they were seated in the kitchen while Ayanna poured cups of fragrant coffee. She was adding cream to hers when Johnny asked her a question.

"Why aren't you married?"

"You don't hold back, do you? Whatever comes up comes out with you." Ayanna picked up her cup to take a sip.

"You're right. I'm very direct. I don't know any other way to be. When I want to know something I ask, and I want to know why a gorgeous, talented, kind woman like you is still single." Johnny tasted his own coffee and made a deep sound of satisfaction. "Let's add 'making coffee' to your list of accomplishments."

"I was engaged once," Ayanna said. "I was engaged my senior year of college, and we were going to get married after I finished at the Cordon Bleu." At his look of surprise, she nodded. "You weren't so far off when you said I cooked like a pro. I majored in business and minored in culinary arts. I got accepted at the Cordon Bleu in Paris, and I would have gone, but my sister died, and I was guardian to my nephews, so my life went down a different path. You know they say if you want to make God laugh, make plans."

Johnny sipped his coffee before asking her another question.

"What happened to your sister, that is, if you don't mind talking about it?"

She met Johnny's concerned gaze with a steady one of her own. "I can tell you about it because it happened

54   *A Case for Romance*

ten years ago. My sister had been in a very unhappy relationship for a long time. She had finally had enough,
and she was in the process of leaving him. He followed
her into the parking structure at her job and killed her,
and then he blew his own brains out. He did it," she said
bitterly, "because he loved her so much."

"I'm so sorry for your loss," Johnny said as he put
his hand over hers. "Do the boys know how their
parents died?"

"No, they don't. I can't bring myself to tell them yet.
If ever. They think it was a car accident. That's why I
moved here, so we could have a fresh start. My sister
was living in Atlanta, and even though they had their
school and their friends, I didn't want them to hear the
news on TV or hear local gossip. I had a friend who was
going to grad school here, and she helped me find a job.
I put the insurance money into a trust fund for their edu-
cations, and here we are. I never did go to cooking
school, but what I did do was a lot better, I think."

They sat in silence for a moment, and then Johnny
asked her another candid question. "What happened to
your fiancé? I'm assuming you never got married."

"No, we didn't. After my sister died, he announced
that he didn't intend to raise somebody else's kids, and
it was them or him. So I passed on him."

"It was his loss," Johnny said.

"And my narrow escape."

Alec and Cameron came in the back door, talking
some trash about their favorite athletes. "Hey, Ma. Is
there anything to eat?"

"You know what's in there. Help yourself, and leave the kitchen clean," she said fondly. "It's getting to be about that time, isn't it?" she said, looking meaningfully at the clock. She insisted that they go to bed at a decent hour for school.

"Not too much longer, Ma," Cameron answered. "Can we get you something, John?"

"Not a thing. Thanks for your hospitality, guys. Don't forget Dave & Buster's this week. Can I persuade you to walk me to the door?" Johnny stood up and held his hand out to Ayanna.

"I think I have just about enough strength in my frail little body to do that."

When they reached the front door, Johnny took both her hands and looked down at her. "Ayanna, this was one of the best days I've had in a long time. And being the greedy person we both know I am, I want more days just like this one. I want to spend more time with you and Alec and Cameron. I want to get to know you better so I can start checking off that list," he said grinning. "Can we do that?"

Ayanna cleared her throat before answering, trying to think of something to say that would be lighthearted and noncommittal. "Sure, that sounds like fun. Just give me a call sometime, okay?"

Johnny pulled her closer to his body as he placed her hands on his shoulders. He leaned in to give her a kiss, and she automatically turned her head to accept a brotherly peck on the cheek. He turned her face so he could touch his lips to hers and brought her even closer so that they were body to body, separated only by the clothes they wore. He covered her mouth with his own and teased her lips apart with his tongue. In seconds the kiss deepened and sweetened into something that Ayanna had never experienced before.

She was blazing hot from the soles of her feet to the top of her head, and her arms were locked around his neck. He was holding her as tightly as he could without hurting her, but even in her hazy state Ayanna didn't care about anything but being closer to him. He lifted her off the floor, and she fit against him even better. His lips were as tasty as dark chocolate and just as sweet. His tongue was doing things to hers that was making her body hungry for more. He nibbled at her full, pouty mouth and suckled the sharp sensation away while drinking her in so deeply that her flip-flops fell off her feet, and she didn't realize it until he gently lowered her to the floor, giving her little kisses as they pulled apart with great reluctance.

"I wanted to make sure there were no misunderstandings, Ayanna. I don't want to be your big brother, your play cousin, your pal or your buddy. I want to be your man."

Ayanna's face reflected her utter surprise, and Johnny had to tease her a little.

"You called it, baby. I don't hold back. Can you handle that?"

Before she could answer him, he was kissing her again, and the need for conversation vanished for the moment.

Chapter 6

Johnny knew he'd behaved brashly, but there was no going back. And he wasn't about to let her hide from him. After he kissed her totally senseless, he called her. He didn't wait until he got to Billie and Jason's house; he called from his cell phone.

He smiled when he heard her voice. "Are you scared of me now?" he teased.

"Yes!"

He laughed at her gently. "You have no reason to be. I meant every word I said, Ayanna. I want you."

"Oh...."

Johnny tried hard not to laugh again. "Look, I know this seems a little hasty—"

"Ya think?"

"Okay, I'll grant you that my behavior may seem a bit precipitous, but I don't believe in wasting time. Do you like me?"

He could hear a little sigh from her end. "Of course I do. You're a very nice man."

"Ouch. If you still think I'm nice after the way I kissed you, I wasn't doing it right."

There it was; the little giggle he loved to hear. "It's been awhile, but you did it just right."

He was immediately intrigued. "How long is 'a while'?"

"Almost ten years," she answered.

"Not since your fiancé?" He tried not to sound incredulous, but it was impossible to keep the shock to himself.

"That's right."

He didn't respond right away, and it was her turn to tease him. "Are you scared of me now?"

"Not in the least, baby. I was just thinking about what fools men can be, that's all. Do you date much?"

"I have two growing sons, a full-time job and I do volunteer work. I don't have time to date."

"I see. Well, get a new planner or PDA or whatever because that's about to change."

When he reached the house, he wasn't surprised to find Billie and his mother waiting for him. He entered the dining room to find them sitting next to each other looking over some catalogs of what seemed to be baby things. They looked at him expectantly, and he crossed his arms and looked back.

"Go ahead, get it over with."

"What are you talking about, Son?"

"That innocent voice doesn't fool me. You're dying to know what happened with Ayanna today, and I'm not going to tell you."

Lee sniffed and went back to her catalog. "He was always a difficult child."

Billie just smirked at him. "I'll see her at work tomorrow, and I'll find out," she said cheerfully.

"You do that. Let me know what she says." He left the room and grinned when he heard her go "Humph."

His father, Boyd, and Jason were watching CNN in the media room, and he sat down to join them. Boyd waited a few minutes before turning to Johnny.

"You had a good time with that young lady, didn't you?"

"The best."

"Good. She's a keeper."

"I agree."

"That's because I'm always right."

Johnny decided to let that one pass. "Pop, how did you know you were going to marry Mama?"

"That's easy. I knew when she told me."

He and Jason slapped hands while Johnny just shook his head.

"I'm going to bed. It's been a long day, and I've got to get ready for the new office," Johnny said as he rose to leave the room.

He detoured through the dining room and whispered to Billie, "Where's the piranha?"

"Davina took an early flight back to New York. You're safe."

"Thank you, Jesus."

As soon as Ayanna got to work, she found Billie waiting for her with a big cup of herbal tea and a cheesy grin on her face. "Here you go," she said sweetly. "It's herbal and decaf because that's all I can have, but it should work."

"Work for what?"

"I'm hoping it'll lubricate your jaws because you know how nosy I am! Did you have fun with Johnny?"

Ayanna put her canvas briefcase on her desk, followed by her purse. She sat down and took the steaming cup from Billie. "You are nosy. Johnny warned me that you were going to snoop," she said, enjoying the look of surprise on Billie's face.

"He told you? When did he tell you?"

"This morning. He called me to say good morning, and he warned me to expect an inquisition."

Billie's eyes widened with admiration. "He never calls women in the morning. Ever. That's definitely a first. So did y'all have a good time or what?"

Ayanna put her cup down and held out her hand to Billie. "Give me your little finger," she demanded.

Billie complied, hooking her pinkie with Ayanna's in the time-honored girlfriend's vow.

"Okay, you can't lie to me. Is your brother crazy?"

"Nope. He's one of the most levelheaded, responsible, caring people in the world. In the universe, really."

"I was afraid of that," Ayanna said glumly. She let go of Billie's finger.

"I'm lost. You find out he's sane, and that scares you?"

"Yes, it does. I haven't been out with a man or been with a man since I broke up with my fiancé. Johnny is a wonderful person. He's very sweet and kind and handsome and he likes my boys and it's just too much for me to take in."

Billie's eyes softened, and she took Ayanna's hand. "I have a question for you. How do you eat an elephant?"

"What?" Ayanna looked and sounded bewildered.

"It's a riddle," Billie explained. "How do you eat an elephant?"

"I have no idea," Ayanna replied.

"One bite at a time. Don't try and figure everything out all at once. I tease my brother a lot because he's always been a ladies' man, but he's a *good* man. Just enjoy yourself."

Enjoying herself proved to be easier than she antici-pated, because Johnny made it so. He called her often, and they had long talks that were both funny and sexy. He took her out several times, always including Alec and Cameron. They went to restaurants and movies and to a baseball game and every outing was more fun than the last. In addition to getting to know him better, Ayanna got a fabulous dessert every time in the form of his divine kisses. On the one hand, she wasn't dreaming about the imaginary Ramon anymore, but her days and nights were full of fantasies about a real man—Johnny.

They were going on a date that night, just the two of them. Alec and Cameron were going to their best friend's house for an end-of-school cookout, and Johnny was taking her for an early dinner.

"Ma, are you ready? John is here to pick you up." Cameron's voice floated up the stairs.

"Tell him he's early! I'll be down in a minute." She wasn't dressed up, but she looked nice. She was wearing jeans and a red halter top in a lustrous rayon knit with a matching shrug to cover her shoulders. Her hair was blown straight, and she had curled it with a one-inch iron for a different look. She had on little makeup, just a powder foundation, mascara and lip gloss. She picked up her clutch bag from the bed and slid her feet into a pair of sexy sandals with three-inch heels. She put another dab of lotion on her hands and her neck so the scent would last, and she was ready to go.

"You look beautiful, as always."

They were seated in a secluded booth in a bistro with a nice atmosphere and a great jazz trio. Ayanna propped her chin in her hand and looked at Johnny. "Thank you. And you look very handsome. Are you still sure you want to make that twelve-hour drive with us?"

"I wouldn't have it any other way." Johnny crossed his arms on the table and gave her one of his long, searching looks.

"It's really nice of you. I've driven it lots of times, though, and we do just fine."

The drive was the distance between Chicago and Columbia, South Carolina, where her mother lived. Alec and Cameron were going to spend the summer with their grandmother and their aunt, and Johnny volunteered to drive down with them.

"I'm sure you do, but you don't have to do things like that by yourself anymore. I wouldn't feel comfortable with you driving by yourself with the boys. People are too crazy these days. It's not like back in the day when it was safe to go on the road. Gas prices have people freaked out; people are scared about losing their jobs…" He stopped talking when Ayanna put her hand over his mouth.

"Wow. Don't hold back. Tell me how you really feel," she said lightly. A soft sound escaped her lips when his tongue stroked her palm. She felt the sensation radiating up her arm and down through her chest right to her nipples. She pulled her hand back and picked up her glass of water.

"I apologize for sounding like your father, but I can't apologize for being concerned about you. Besides, a road trip can be a lot of fun. It'll give us time to work on your list."

"Will you stop with that list? I haven't given you a list of my desires." She made a little face at him.

"I'm going to make one for you. Are you a virgin?"

Ayanna rolled her eyes. "Nice segue, chief. No, I'm not a virgin. I haven't had a lot of experience, but I've had some."

"But not since your engagement," he said.

"That's a big assumption. Who says it's been that long?"

"You did," he reminded her.

Ayanna bit her lower lip. "Okay, you got me."

"How have you gone so long without intimacy? People need that closeness, that contact. It's part of what makes us human." Johnny took one of her hands and started rubbing his thumb on the back of it, stroking it softly but firmly.

"Really? Well, not everybody thinks that sex is the be-all and end-all. I didn't think it was all that great."

The soft stroking of her hand continued. "That's because he didn't do it right. What was his name, anyway?"

Ayanna's palm was moist and warm, and she was feeling that same heady damp heat in other parts of her body as she looked into his hypnotic eyes. "His name was, umm, Percy."

"Well, Percy didn't know what the hell he was doing. You're a very sensual woman, and you need a man who appreciates every inch of you and knows how to bring you the kind of pleasure you were meant to feel."

She pulled her hand away quickly and used it to fan her face. "Whoa. Does that line usually work for you?"

"I can't say, I've never said those words to a woman before. But I have to say I've never met a woman who needed to hear them more than you."

His words rang in her ears all the way back to her

house. They barely spoke on the way, and she was still distracted when they reached her door. She tried twice to insert the key in the lock and failed.

"Let me do that for you." He took the keys from her and opened the door. After they were inside, he looked around the house to make sure everything was secure. Ayanna followed him down the hall to the spare room and watched as he checked the windows.

He turned to see her standing in the doorway and held out his hand.

She walked to him slowly and took his hand. He sat down on the chaise and pulled her into his lap. "Did I embarrass you at the restaurant?"

"A little. I was more excited than embarrassed," she mumbled into his shoulder.

"That's good." He kissed her hair, her forehead and tilted her chin up so he could kiss her mouth. It was slow and tender at first, his tongue teasing the edge of her lips. He sucked gently until her mouth opened to receive him. Her hands moved to his shoulders, and she held on tight as a strange sensation took over her body. She felt an urgency building between her legs, and she wanted to get closer to Johnny, wanted to feel him on her and in her. Suddenly everything came to a head, and she tensed, moaning his name out loud as she felt a convulsive shock of pure bliss.

Only when their lips came apart did she realize that he'd somehow freed her breasts from her strapless bra and was stroking them, his thumbs circling her nipples and making her crazy with desire.

"He never did that to you, did he?"

Ayanna couldn't speak; she was too amazed by what had just happened. He moved so that she was straddling him on the chaise while he took off her shrug and slid the top and bra down to free her breasts. He bent his head to her nipples and stroked one with his hot tongue before taking it in his mouth like a piece of his favorite candy. He sucked and licked one, then the other until that amazing feeling took over again, and she was rocking her hips against his massive erection and stifling a scream.

All too soon, he released her and pulled her top back up. He was still holding her and his lips were still warming her throat and her collarbone, but now the quivering and throbbing were going on deep in her womanly recesses, and she didn't want them to stop.

"Shh, it's okay, baby. I shouldn't have done that, but I wanted you to see that it can be that good. I'm not going to have the boys come home and find me pawing you so we have to stop, even though it's the last thing I want to do. But when we're on our way back from South Carolina, you're all mine, every sweet inch of you. And I'm going to show you what loving is all about."

Her eyes were glazed as she continued to gently rock against his manhood. "You mean there's more?"

He kissed her hard, cupping her face in his hands. "There's a whole lot more, and we're going to love every minute of it."

Chapter 7

When they pulled up in the driveway of the beautiful two-story home of Lucie Porter, Johnny felt right at home. The house was as gracious and warm as Ayanna's mother, who made him feel welcome as soon as she greeted her doting grandsons.

"Cameron and Alec! I thought you'd never get here," she exclaimed. "Come give me some sugar, you two." The boys ran to her open arms and embraced her willingly.

"I practically have to sit on them to get that much love," Ayanna said laughingly. "Hey, Mommy, I'm here, too, or did you not see me?"

Lucie came down the porch steps with a big smile. "Of course I see you, sweetie. How could I not see my baby?" She threw her arms open for a big hug, and Ayanna took it gratefully. They hugged tightly and Lucie said, "You look beautiful, honey, just gorgeous. Have a real glow about you."

Finally it was Johnny's turn. "Johnny, this is my mother, Lucie Porter. Mommy, this is Johnny," Ayanna said shyly.

Johnny took the hand Lucie extended to him and kissed it. "Mrs. Porter, it's an absolute privilege to meet you," he said.

"The pleasure is all mine. And call me Lucie," she said, taking his arm. "I have a feeling we're going to be very good friends. You all can get the luggage later. I've fixed you a little something to eat, and we can get acquainted."

The interior of the house was mid-century modern but uniquely Lucie with pops of color against the neutral palette. The furniture was oyster-white, but there were bright pillows and paintings and healthy green plants everywhere. It reminded Johnny of Ayanna's home, very feminine and warm. Lucie was almost as good a cook as Ayanna, and she'd made a feast of braised short ribs, macaroni and cheese, hot homemade rolls, fresh okra and tomatoes and green beans. The boys ate like they hadn't seen food in weeks, and Johnny wasn't far behind.

"Lucie, this was delicious," he said. "I can see where Ayanna got her skill."

"Oh, honey, that's sweet of you, but Ayanna actually taught me a few things. She really learned to cook from her great-grandmother and my mother. She used to love to be in the kitchen with Nonnie, my grandmother.

She would sit on a big stool and watch everything she did, and by the time she was five or six, she was helping her bake cookies and make piecrust. She was fascinated by everything that went on in the kitchen. I knew she'd be a chef one day," Lucie said fondly.

They were sitting in the dining room sipping Lucie's delicious sweet tea and letting their meal digest. The boys had gallantly cleared the table and started the dishwasher before taking off to explore the yard and shoot some hoops.

"Johnny, I can't thank you enough for bringing my family home safely. That was so kind of you," Lucie said. She seemed to be taking his measure as she spoke, and she liked what she saw.

"It wasn't kind at all," Johnny said, caressing Ayanna with his eyes. "I didn't want her driving that far by herself. I wanted to make sure she and the boys got here okay. There're a lot of loony tunes out there these days."

"Very gallant," Lucie murmured.

Johnny had a question that surprised Ayanna. "So why did you always think she'd be a chef and not a dancer? Where did she learn to dance like she does?"

Ayanna groaned. "So, the garden looks really nice," she said loudly, hoping to change the subject, but it was too late.

"Honey, my baby started dancing in the womb," Lucie said. "If there was music on, she'd start kicking and jumping until it went off! When she was a baby she danced before she could walk. Come on in the living room, and let me show you some pictures."

"I'm going to call Emily. Johnny, don't let her start showing movies or we're leaving tonight," she threatened.

Johnny was enthralled by the pictures of Ayanna as an adorable dimpled baby, a charming toddler and the prettiest little girl he'd ever seen. Most of the pictures showed her with long curly hair, and she looked like a doll. All her dance recital pictures were there, and they were so unbearably cute he couldn't stand it. Ayanna came into the living room to report that her sister Emily hadn't answered her phone.

"I left her a message. Mommy, don't show him those," she protested.

"Too late," Johnny said. "You were a beautiful baby, and you're an even more beautiful woman. Don't be embarrassed."

She went to the sofa where he was sitting with Lucie and sat down next to him. He put his arm around her and kissed her on the cheek. "You could have been a professional dancer, you know."

"It was fun, but it was never my passion," she said simply. "I like feeding people more."

He whispered in her ear, "You can feed me anytime you want."

Lucie smiled and pretended that she didn't notice a thing.

"Why do all men think they have to do the grilling?" Ayanna was smiling as she looked out her mother's kitchen window. Johnny was explaining to Alec and

Cameron all the finer points of turning out perfectly done barbecue.

"Honey, it's a man thing, that's all I can tell you. They might not be able to boil water, but hand them a slab of raw meat and an open flame and they go right back to being cavemen. Can you do me a favor and put some eggs on for the potato salad?"

"Hmm? Oh, I made it already. It's in the refrigerator," Ayanna said absentmindedly.

"Oh, thank you, honey. You're still Mama's sweetie pie. Now, do you think you can tear yourself away from the window before you wear your eyes out looking at that big hunk of man?"

Ayanna turned to give her mother a big cheese-eating grin. The resemblance between the two was evident in the color of their skin and their big dimples, as well as their long curly eyelashes. Lucie Porter was a little shorter than Ayanna, and her layered hair was shoulder-length. It was streaked with rich chestnut-brown, and she had the same slender build as her daughter.

"I'm trying to, but I can't seem to stop."

Lucie laughed. "He is awfully pretty. I'd look at him, too, if he was mine. Tell me again, what does he do for a living?"

Tearing her eyes away at last, Ayanna went to the freezer to take out some of the peaches her mother put up every summer. "I think I'll make a cobbler." While she was getting the flour and butter and sugar, she reminded her mother about Johnny's occupation.

"He's a lawyer. He used to be in labor law, but he left that to head up an international relief foundation that does work all over the world. He travels to Africa a lot and to other places, too. He's very compassionate, and the boys are so taken with him! He likes to spend time with them."

"I can tell. It's about time you—" Lucie's words were cut off by the banging of the back door.

"About time she got a man, Mother?"

Ayanna and Lucie exchanged a look as the youngest member of the Porter family, Emily, came in the kitchen wearing her customary deadpan expression. She continued talking in a sneering tone. "Ooh, let's have a parade because Ayanna done found her a man! 'Cause Lawd knows that's all a woman is good for. Got to get her a good man and settle down to start pumpin' out babies."

Emily bore little resemblance to her mother or sister. She was five-foot-eight and a good bit heavier than either woman. She would have been attractive, but she made no effort with her appearance or her attitude. It was a hot, sunny day, and she was wearing denim overalls and a long-sleeved henley shirt with thick-soled boots. Her hair was thick and long, but it was dry and unruly, and the way she had it pulled back into a sloppy ponytail did nothing to emphasize her features. All it did was give her an angry look because she had a rather low hairline.

"Hello, Emily. It's nice to see you. Thanks again for inviting the boys to your science camp." Ayanna did what she almost always had to do with Emily, which was change the subject and act as though she hadn't heard any rudeness.

Emily gave her a mean little grin. "Oh no, you're not going to go all passive-aggressive on me. I did my thesis on that crap."

"Which one of the three?" Ayanna murmured as she washed her hands. Emily had so many degrees Ayanna had lost count. She was a college professor and apparently a good one because her students loved her and she enjoyed the respect of her peers. Ayanna was quite proud of her younger sister, but they weren't very close. Emily's prickly personality made it impossible for anyone to get close to her.

"So who's the loser you've hooked yourself up with?"

"I don't know any losers," Ayanna said. "But that's my friend John Phillips at the grill, and if you'd like to meet him, the boys will be happy to do the honors." She began measuring the ingredients for her pastry crust to show Emily that this particular conversation was over. She was in too good a mood to let her sister upset her. But Emily got the last word.

"I would like to meet him. I'd love to see what all the fuss is about." She turned around and headed for the back door.

The two days they spent in Columbia went quickly. Johnny thoroughly enjoyed meeting Ayanna's family, especially her mother, who was as charming and personable as Ayanna. He glanced over to the passenger seat where Ayanna had her nose buried in a book. She was wearing red shorts with a white blouse, and her little black flats with the red bow on the toes were, even to his male eye, too cute. The best part of her ensemble was the shorts, however. He could look at her fantastic legs as much as he wanted, and even better, he could touch them, which he did. He reached over and stroked the warm silky skin of her thigh, waiting for her response.

She didn't let him down; she went "ooh" before the adorable little giggle followed.

"Are you trying to give me a heart attack? I'll give you exactly fifteen minutes to stop that."

He stroked her again and kept his hand on her leg. "Did you have a good time, baby?"

"I always do. My mom and I are very close, so it's always good to see her. She thinks you're a magnificent specimen of man, by the way. That's a direct quote."

"Aw, you're gonna make me blush. The feeling is mutual, though. Your mother is a goddess," he said. "She reminds me of my mother. They're even in the same profession."

Like Lee Phillips, Lucie Porter had started as an RN but kept taking classes until she got two masters degrees and started teaching nursing. Now both of them were college department heads. Johnny had a feeling the two women would really hit it off, although he knew no such thing would happen with sister Emily. With his usual frankness, he asked Ayanna a question.

"About Emily. Does she hate all men, or is it just me?"

A long sigh came from Ayanna. "Look, don't take it personally. There aren't too many people she likes, regardless of gender. She's an equal-opportunity hater. She dislikes men, women, cats, children, old people, young people, rainy days, sunny days, vegetarians, meat eaters, whatevers. She's just not real sociable," she said. "I don't know how she got to be so crabby at such a young age. She was really close to Daddy, and when he died it was very hard on her. It was hard on all of us, but she was the worst."

Johnny continued stroking her thigh, because he loved the feel of her and because he wanted to impart some comfort to her.

"Sometimes I think that's why Mommy never dated again. There are any number of men who've wanted to get closer to her, but she keeps them all at arm's length. I think it's because of Emily. She would pitch such an unholy fit whenever a man would come around that Mommy just quit trying to have a normal life. Even now that Emily lives on her own and has a career, Mommy is still single and unattached. But I think she'd really like to have a man in her life."

Her paperback book slid to the floor, and she dove after it.

"What the heck are you reading? I'm taking you to one of the most romantic cities in the South for some alone time, and you're reading a book on the way?" He shook his head.

"Aw, now don't get pouty. I'm very excited about going to Charleston. It's a beautiful place, and it was very thoughtful of you to think of it. But I'm not really reading, I'm studying."

On the night of their date, before Johnny left to pick up the boys from their friend's party, he'd announced that he was kidnapping her. "Since we're going all the way to South Carolina, I'm taking you to Charleston for a couple of days. Do you like Charleston?"

"I love it, but—"

"Take that word out of your vocabulary, Ayanna. I want us to be someplace unique, beautiful and private when we make love for the first time. You deserve the best, and I'm going to give it to you, always."

Two days later they left for South Carolina, and now they were on their way for the first vacation Ayanna had ever taken with a man. And she called herself studying?

"What in the world could be so important that you have to bone up on it now?"

Ayanna showed him the cover of the book, which depicted a handsome man and a very sexy-looking woman locked in a passionate embrace. "I'm brushing up on my technique," she said mischievously.

"You read those things? Is that porn or something?"

Ayanna shook her head vigorously. "No, this is not porn. I love romance novels, I always have. Mommy used to read them, and I used to steal hers. These are regular novels, but they're just really sexy and exciting."

"Baby, you are looking at all the excitement you need right here," Johnny said.

"I'm sure I am, darlin'. But I'm the neophyte, remember?"

"Read it to me. I want to see what some writer thinks passes for real grown and sexy romance."

"Okay."

She began reading in the voice that drove him crazy. She had a low, sexy way of speaking that made him melt inside, and when she got to the love scenes he almost drove off the expressway.

"What's up, chief? You want me to stop reading?"

"Hell, no. Keep going, baby. This is hot."

"Just remember, you asked for this." She kept reading until he finally said enough.

"All right, Ayanna, that's enough. That's like audio erotica. I had no idea that's what those books were like. It's got a good plot, the characters were real and the sex was, well, let's just say it was inspiring."

"Do you mean that, or are you just trying to humor me?"

He took her hand in his and placed it over his thigh so she could feel his erection. It was rock-hard and ready for business.

"I'm not trying to humor anybody. I'm trying to get to the hotel before I pull off the road and do something real crazy."

Ayanna's eyes got big as she realized the length and width of him. "Um, Johnny? Hurry up, please."

He gave a harsh, short laugh and glanced at the dashboard clock. "We'll be there in about twenty minutes. Ten if you don't move your hand."

He laughed again as she snatched her hand back like his pants had burst into flames.

"Johnny, this isn't what I expected at all."

"Don't you like it here?" He sounded a little bit apprehensive, and she quickly assured him that she loved it.

"Oh, I love it, but I thought we'd be going to a hotel. This place is like something out of a movie. It's amazing." She was standing in the living room of their villa at the Wild Dunes Resort on the Isle of Palms. It was about a half hour from Charleston, and it was magnificent. The living room had a modern yet tropical feel with warm earth colors and every possible creature comfort. A small kitchen and two bedrooms with baths completed the cottage.

Johnny crossed the room and put his hands on her hips. "Did you think I was going to take you to some no-tell motel? You should know me better than that. You only get the best, baby. And I didn't want to keep our neighbors up since I think you're gonna be loud."

She opened her mouth for an indignant retort and got a mouthful of joy for her efforts. He covered her lips with his and kissed her until she was breathless. "I'm not loud," she whispered.

"Yes, but you will be." Still holding her hips, he pulled her closer, stroking and squeezing her butt. "Did I ever tell you what a cute bottom you have?"

"Actually, no, you've never mentioned it." She put her hands on his behind and moved them up and down.

"Are you hungry?" He lifted her up, and she had to put her arms on his shoulders for balance.

"No, I'm not."

"Tired?"

"Not at all."

"Want to take a shower?"

Ayanna nodded her head before putting one hand on each side of his face. "Yes, I do. With you," she said before kissing him gently. He lifted her higher, and she wrapped her legs around his waist and kept kissing him until they were in the bedroom.

Somehow he managed to get her on the bed and lay down on top of her without breaking the kiss. She loved feeling his weight and his warmth so close to her, but it didn't last long because he rolled over on his back, taking her with him. Now she was on his chest, looking down at him.

"You're really strong, aren't you?"

"You don't weigh that much. I could carry you all day. But right now, I want to get you out of these clothes." He was trying to unbutton the small buttons on her blouse.

She rose to her knees and took over, undoing one button at a time until the blouse was undone, and she removed it.

"You can unhook my bra," she offered.

"Thank you," he said. He sat up and kissed her flat, toned stomach, licking her navel while he tried to unhook the bra from the back. "How do you undo this thing?"

"See this little flower in front? That's the hook."

The words were barely out of her mouth before he'd released it and her breasts were bared to his welcoming eyes. "Those are the prettiest... Mmm," he took one in his mouth while he slid the bra off her body.

"Your turn. We're supposed to be taking a shower, remember?" She wasn't aware that her voice was shaking a little, but Johnny heard it.

He pulled away from her long enough to stand up and take off his shirt while he kicked off his loafers, and then he unbuckled his belt and unzipped his jeans. Ayanna felt a warmth building between her thighs, and her nipples were already engorged from his brief play. He was beautiful, in every sense of the word. His dark skin gleamed in the afternoon sunlight, and when he pulled down his briefs and jeans in one motion, she could see the full length of his arousal. Her eyes widened and her mouth formed an O of awe.

"I'm not going to hurt you, baby. It's not as big as it looks."

Ayanna looked at him with a sexy smile. "Oh yes it is. And I want it," she murmured.

She unfastened her shorts and took them off with Johnny's help. Her thong followed, and before she knew it, he was carrying her to the shower.

Chapter 8

The warm water felt wonderful but not as good as it felt to be in Johnny's arms. His strong, muscular arms were locked around her waist, and she stood on tiptoe to get closer to him. He lifted her so that she was resting on his erection, and the heavy thickness of it made her tremble. "Johnny," she moaned.

"I'm right here, baby." He gently slid her down so she was facing him. He reached for a bottle of bath gel and put some in his palm. He poured out some of the lightly scented liquid and rubbed it on her breasts. "You are so pretty. These are perfect," he told her. "Everything about you is perfect." She was holding his waist while he rubbed her body in circles, making a soft lather that felt heavenly. "Turn around," he said.

She did, holding her arms up so he could lather every inch of her body, making a soft sound of pleasure when he started palming her buttocks. He knelt down and kissed each one, lavishing her tender skin with his tongue. This time he didn't say anything, but he turned her to face him.

He applied more gel to her body, this time concentrating on the silky triangle that covered her womanhood. One of the two handheld showerheads was on the floor of the tub next to him, and he picked it up, using it to rinse away the foam. It was a wonderful sensation, but not as good as what came next. He gripped her hips and positioned his head so that he could kiss the inside of her thighs, licking his way to the treasure. His tongue was deep between her legs, stroking her femininity and caressing the throbbing pearl, sucking and licking until the pleasure got to be too much to hold in. She cried out but he didn't relent; he kept going while she climaxed again and again.

He gradually slowed down, finishing in one long, passionate caress that left tears rolling down her face. She collapsed onto him, and he held her tightly. He lifted the lever that stopped the tub and it began to fill with warm foamy water. "Happy?"

He was leaning back against the high, broad tub, and she was lying on his chest. Small aftershocks rippled through her, and she felt amazing, lighter-than-air, dreamy and satisfied. "Yes, I am. Are you?"

"Better than that." He put his lips to her ear and whispered, "You were so worth the wait."

Ayanna was looking around for the bath gel, and

when she found it, it was her turn to bathe him. She straddled his long legs and started rubbing his broad chest with the foaming gel. She loved touching him, loved the feel of his skin. She leaned forward to lick the base of his throat, and it tasted so good she kept doing it, stroking and licking until she got to his nipples. She treated them just like he'd treated hers, kissing and sucking until she heard a long groan.

Looking really pleased with herself she sat up and said, "Don't you like that?"

"Don't play with me," he said sternly. "You know I like that."

"How about this?" She moved so that she was sitting down in the tub facing him, and she took his manhood in both hands. "You might have to teach me how to do this," she confessed as she stroked it gently, moving her hands up and down the hard shaft. "I'm not very good at this kind of thing," she added.

"You're doing just fine," he assured her.

He was caught off guard when she lowered her head and covered the tip with her mouth. Her tongue circled it gently and tentatively at first, but she parted her lips wider and increased the pressure as she continued to stroke the shaft.

"Ayanna, oh damn, Ayanna." His voice was hoarse, and his breathing had quickened. "Slow down, baby. Come up here. Stop, stop," he groaned.

She allowed him to gather her into his arms although she protested. "Was I doing it wrong?"

"You were doing it way too well. I'm trying to make

this all about you, and I want it to last all night, so we just need to slow down or… Well, never mind. So is that what you've learned from those novels of yours?"

"Yep. I'm a quick study."

He stood up, taking her with him. He wrapped a towel around her before putting one on himself. "Sweetness, you're the valedictorian of your class. Get me that author's address, I want to send her some orchids," he said as he carried her into their bedroom.

He set her on the bed like she was a precious work of very fragile art. Her hair was wet from the shower, and it was already forming curls around her face. Her makeup, what little she wore, was gone. Her skin was dewy and moist and he wanted to lick all the droplets of water from every bit of her body. He spread a dry towel over the bedspread, and then he pulled the pillows out. He lay down and smiled when Ayanna joined him. She leaned over to kiss him.

"My hair is wet," she murmured.

"So? You're still gorgeous," he replied as he undid the towel to reveal her body.

She returned the favor, undoing the thick terry cloth to reveal his thickening desire for her.

"I thought you'd be shy," he said, smiling as she wrapped her small hand around his tumescence.

"I thought I would be, too. Maybe I'm a hoochie at heart and never knew it." She was stroking him up and down, slowly and deliberately. Her arousal was evident in the way her nipples were beginning to harden and grow larger. He leaned over to take one in his mouth and sucked hard, making her moan softly. Her free hand began rubbing the back of his head, spreading a soft fire down his back. He pulled harder, making her arch her back and whisper his name. He wanted her to feel even more, and using his long fingers, he found the source of her pleasure and began to stroke until she felt wet and hot, ready for more.

He used his thumb to stroke her pulsing clitoris, moving in circles to increase the sensation while he moved his mouth to her other breast, applying the same strong suction. Her hand trembled then tightened on his fully engorged penis, and he could feel the beginning of her climax. Her hips were moving, and her breaths were coming rapidly. He kissed his way up her chest to her neck, then to her lips. He kissed her open mouth and looked at her face as her eyes fluttered closed and her body responded to his touch. When her release came, it was long and gratifying, and the sounds of satisfaction were music to his ears.

He was going to ease her down on the bed to rest, but she surprised him again. "I want to make love to you, Johnny. I want to make you feel what you do to me," she whispered. "Kiss me, please."

He did so at once, tasting her, sucking and licking her lips until he had to stop to get the condoms or risk putting his baby into her. He retrieved them quickly, and she insisted that he let her do it. He lay back and watched her apply it, slowly and carefully. He loved looking at her, especially now with her legs spread over him and her body moist and ready.

"Have you ever done it like this?"

Her eyes widened. "On top?"

"Yes. You're going to get on top of me, and we're going to take it slow and easy until you're ready for more." He slid his hands up her thighs and held her hips, helping her balance as he entered her. She closed her eyes and sighed as he began to push slowly, trying to establish an easy rhythm. She moved with him, rocking back and forth, rising and falling with his every thrust. She was tight, hot and wet, and when he felt her muscles clench and flex on his manhood, it was his turn to call her name. He let go of her hips to hold her hands, and with their fingers clasped, they rode out the passionate storm together. He was watching her face again, and when she threw her head back and a low, musical sound came from her throat he let go of her hands and grasped her hips again, holding her tightly as he let out his own release, thrusting up sharply as a sharp cry was torn from his throat.

She fell onto his chest, and he held her close. His heart was pounding as hard as hers, and they were both sweaty and very satisfied. He kissed her every so often and rubbed her back gently. If it had meant his life he couldn't have let her go. He held her until her soft, regular breathing told him she'd fallen asleep, and only then did he close his own eyes.

When Ayanna finally awoke, she was groggy and disoriented. She reached over to touch Johnny, but the bed was empty. She sat up, clutching the sheet to her naked body. *Was I dreaming? Did it really happen or have I finally gone over the edge?* As she started to get out of bed, she felt the pleasant aftermath of their fierce lovemaking, and she knew it wasn't a fantasy. But where was Johnny? The phone on the bedside table rang, and she got her answer.

"Hello, sweetness. I let you sleep, and I went to get us something to eat. I'll be back in about a half hour if you want to take a shower."

"That sounds nice. I'll get up now," she said, covering a dainty yawn.

"How do you feel?" he asked.

"Wonderful. Fabulous. Hungry."

His deep laugh warmed her heart. "I'll see you soon, baby."

She stood up and found that last night she'd used some muscles that hadn't been active for some time, so she decided to take a bath and get rid of the slight soreness. She found her small bag with her cosmetics and took out the rose-scented bubble bath and creamy body wash. Soon the bathroom was filled with the heady scent of roses, and she was soaking in a tub full of bubbles. She amused herself by playing with the jets in the whirlpool tub, and in a short time she felt relaxed and ready for more of Johnny's passionate loving.

He was unlike anyone she'd ever met in her life. And he made her feel like she'd never felt before. He made her feel like a real woman. *What did I do to deserve this?* They always say to be careful what you wish for, and she understood the meaning of the phrase fully, now that all her wishes had come true. For years she'd wished for a prince and now she had a king. Of course, she only had him for a short time, but every minute they were together would be worth the pain she'd endure when their fling was over. He wasn't the marrying kind, and she wasn't the type he'd ever marry. The thought made her catch her breath and massage the area right over her heart. It would kill her to have to give him up when the time came.

"Where are you, baby?"

Hastily wiping her eyes, she cleared her throat. "I'm still in the bathroom."

He opened the door asking if she was decent.

"Not anymore. Come on in," she invited.

"It smells good in here. Here, let me do your back," he offered. He had changed shirts and was wearing a linen one with the sleeves rolled up. He knelt next to the tub and kissed her, then took the bath puff from her hand and put some more body wash on it. He began washing her back as if they were a real couple and he'd done it for years. She stretched like a cat as he soaped her from the nape of her neck down to her rounded derriere.

"Did you sleep well?" he asked.

"Absolutely. When I woke up and you weren't here, I thought it had all been a dream until I realized I wasn't at home," she admitted.

"I should have left you a note. I'm sorry. Next time I will. I just didn't want to wake you because you looked so sweet." He leaned in for another kiss.

"You're sweet," she murmured. "What did you get to eat?"

He was still rubbing her back with one hand, but the other one was making a voyage of its own beneath the suds. "Something that will keep for a while. Want some company?"

"How fast can you get in?"

In less than a minute, he was rid of his clothes and they were entwined in the tub, kissing madly. It was a huge circular tub that could easily hold four adults, making it the perfect size for Johnny's long legs. She made him lie against the bath pillow and began rubbing his chest with her soapy hands.

"I know you're already clean, but I just like the way you feel. I like the way you look, too. You're probably the handsomest man I've ever seen. Better than Ramon." She giggled.

"Who the hell is Ramon?" he demanded.

She laughed at his reaction and at what she was about to reveal to him.

"Ramon was my imaginary lover. I used to dream about him and make up these elaborate fantasies. Isn't that pathetic?"

"What did he look like, this Ramon?" His voice sounded slightly gruff.

"Oh, he was the generic type, typical tall, dark and handsome. I think he had long hair," she said thoughtfully. "To be honest, he was like a composite of all the heroes from my novels. He was just there when I needed him."

She was still massaging him, kneading his firm flesh and reveling in his sheer maleness. He guided her in the water so that she was sitting in his lap. "You're not going to need him anymore," he said firmly. "You got that?"

"I might need some convincing," she teased as her thumbs played with his nipples.

His fingers immediately found her most sensitive spot, and he manipulated it with loving skill until she was throbbing and begging for more.

He relented but only long enough to reach out of the tub to get a condom out of the pocket of the jeans he'd discarded. "Now that I know what a hot little thing you are, I'm always going to be prepared." He quickly sheathed himself, rising to his knees to do so. "Get in front of me, Ayanna. Just like that, but bend over," he urged.

He helped her get into a kneeling position, running his palms up and down her sides and palming her round brown globes. "Hold on to the tub, baby." She put her hands on the rim and had to stifle a scream as she felt him enter her body from behind. Once he was fully inside, he began to pump slowly, in and out. As she got used to the pace, she began to respond and he took her on a ride to paradise. He squeezed her breasts and whispered loving words to her as he thrust his hardness into her softness.

He held her hips and she was spiraling out of control while he continued the ride. When his thumb began to caress her jewel her moans turned to a long cry of passion fulfilled, and his voice joined hers as he stopped pumping and ground his hips into her. She thought it was over but he gently helped her turn to face him. He kissed her rough and hard, then soft and sweet. "I have to see your face, Ayanna. When you come it's the sexiest thing in the world. Come for me now, baby. Let me see it on your face," he coaxed.

Incredibly, he was still hard and she was still yearning for him. He continued to pump and thrust, and she met him stroke for stroke. She held on to his shoulders, and their eyes were linked by the intensity of their desire until the world turned over and she came apart yet again. "That's it, Ayanna, that look on your face. Ayanna…" His words turned to moans, and he roared like a lion as he joined her in ecstasy.

It was much later, after they rinsed off the bubbles and dressed quickly, that Johnny told her something she didn't know. He was wearing another towel, and she had on one of his shirts and nothing else. They were sitting on the sofa in the living room sipping champagne. Johnny had bought a roast chicken, a loaf of French bread, wine, cheese and fruit for dinner. She had just fed him a strawberry, and he'd finished his glass of Cristal champagne. He stretched out on the sofa and put his head in her lap. After they kissed, he gave her a really sweet smile and asked if she knew his middle name.

"No, I don't actually. What is it?"

Grinning like a Cheshire cat he said, "It's Raymond."

"Oh, snap," she said, and they both laughed until the kissing began again.

Chapter 9

The smell of coffee roused Ayanna from sleep. And this time she wasn't alone. Johnny's arm was around her waist, and he was kissing the back of her neck.

"Good morning."

"Good morning to you," she said with a smile. She could feel him cuddled up to her body, but when she put her arm on his she could feel clothes. "Why are you dressed?"

"Because I got up early, took a shower and went to get breakfast. And because I have no intention of wearing you out. We clocked a lot of loving hours yesterday, and I don't want to break you," he said. "I could hurt a little thing like you."

She hurriedly sat up and wished she hadn't. "Ouch."

She looked over her shoulder at Johnny, who was lying on his side, propped up on his elbow. "See? I told you we overdid it yesterday. So today, we're taking it slow and easy. I ran a bath for you, and I brought you breakfast and then you're going to the spa."

"Spa? Really? I've never actually been to one," she said. "That's very thoughtful of you, Johnny." She was looking around for something to cover herself and didn't see a thing.

"Looking for this?" Johnny was holding her silky pink kimono on his index finger.

"Yes, as a matter of fact, I am." She reached for it only to have him pull it away.

"Where's my good morning kiss?"

She covered her mouth with one hand and held out the other. "In the bathroom with my toothpaste and mouthwash, and you should be real happy about that. Gimme."

She slipped on the robe after flashing her perky breasts at him. She stood up and had to stifle a groan. She was feeling pain in body parts she didn't know she had. How could she have felt so wonderful last night and so miserable this morning? She took one small step and then another.

"Aw, baby, let me carry you." Johnny was beside her before she knew it.

"Absolutely not. I'm going to walk into the bathroom with what's left of my dignity, and you are not going to say another word about it," she said. "Not a word."

She did her best to take slow, normal steps, but it was hard. She tightened the robe around her body and bit her lower lip as she hobbled to the door where a hot, scented oasis awaited her. Sighing with relief when she reached the doorway she tossed the robe aside and put one foot in the tub.

"You sure look good from the back, baby." Johnny gave a low whistle.

Ayanna sank into the piles of bubbles and prepared to let the hot water do its work. The bath pillow cradled her neck, and she closed her eyes to relax. She might be stiff as a board today but every minute she and Johnny spent making love was worth it. If she never in her life experienced anything like it again, it was worth it.

She was about to drift off to sleep when Johnny's voice roused her. "You have twenty more minutes, and then I'm coming to get you. If you drown in there, your mother will never forgive me."

"I wouldn't be too happy, either. I'd haunt you for the rest of your days," she said with a laugh. *Just like you're going to stay in my heart forever.*

The spa treatments she received were absolutely wonderful. She got a facial, a mud bath and a wonderful massage that made her feel and look like a new woman. Her hair was shampooed, blown dry and curled, and the makeup artist accentuated her features with a light application of color.

"You have fabulous skin," the woman, whose name

was Candice, praised. "You really don't need much of anything to look good because you have those nice black eyebrows and long eyelashes. I'm just going to put a little highlight under your brows and a gold shadow before I put on the mascara," she murmured. "Then I'm going to give you some bronze blush and a rose-gold lip gloss." She touched Ayanna's face lightly and thoroughly and in a few minutes, she was finished. "There, what do you think?" She turned the chair around so Ayanna could look in the mirror.

Ayanna was pleased with what she saw. She looked good, even to her own eyes. So good, in fact, that she decided to buy a new dress. She went into the boutique next to the spa and found a summery-looking dress of sheer fabric that was patterned with flowers. It had a low back and spaghetti straps, and the skirt flowed out from the flattering empire waist. She was so taken with it that she bought it at once. She was still feeling guilty about it when she got back to the villa, but she put it out of her mind. It was by far the most expensive dress she'd ever purchased, but she wanted to look good for Johnny. They were going to a nice restaurant that night, and she wanted to dazzle him.

Her ploy worked because when she came out of the bedroom dressed for dinner, he had to take a deep breath.

"Every time I think I know exactly what you look like, you surprise me. I thought I knew what beauty was, but you surpass everything I've ever seen," he said.

The look in his eyes made Ayanna want to cry, but

she swallowed hard and tried to give him a lighthearted response. "If you're trying to get out of feeding me, you can forget it," she said.

He ignored her quip and leaned down to kiss her gently on the lips. "Just beautiful."

The restaurant he'd chosen was called Middleton Place. It was a historic landmark that boasted gardens, a stable and museum. They arrived early so they could walk through the gardens before their meal. Ayanna loved the feel of the warm air on her bare shoulders as they roamed through the exquisite gardens. They walked hand in hand looking at the carefully cultivated flowers. To be more accurate, Ayanna looked at the flowers while Johnny looked at her. That was why they didn't see the guided missile headed their way.

"John Phillips! What are you doing in Charleston?"

The high-pitched female voice pierced the restful aura of their solitude. Ayanna saw a tall, thin woman with enormous breasts heading their way and she froze. She was pushed to the side like a swinging door as the woman latched on to Johnny. She was babbling a mile a minute, completely ignoring Ayanna's presence.

"It's been so long," she gushed. "I haven't seen you since that weekend in Capetown! How have you been, you handsome thing?"

Johnny took his time in answering. He took his handkerchief out of his jacket and wiped her bright lipstick off his face like it was snail slime. "Hello, Peyton." Putting his arm around Ayanna's waist, he anchored her next to his body. "Ayanna, this is Peyton Smith. Peyton, this," he said, looking down at Ayanna, "is Ayanna Porter."

Ayanna returned the woman's phony smile with one of her own. She could feel the woman assessing her, and she sensed the exact moment the other woman decided she was no competition.

"So nice to meet you, Alana." She turned the full power of her silicone chest on Johnny and started to ask him about some conference, but Johnny cut her off.

"If you'll excuse us, our table is ready. Nice seeing you," he said as they walked away.

Despite that interlude, the evening was lovely. She appreciated the fact that Johnny cleared up any potential misunderstanding about Peyton. "You'll have to excuse her. She's obviously full of herself, which is why she deliberately mispronounced your name. She's the president of a pharmaceutical company, and I met her a couple of years ago. That weekend in Capetown she was referring to was just two people at a conference who went their separate ways afterward. Period. This is the first time I've seen her since then."

"I believe you. You didn't have to explain, but I'm glad you did," she replied.

"How did you know? Have you got some psychic abilities you haven't told me about?" Johnny looked at her over the rim of his glass.

"All women are psychic. It's part of our charm. But if you must know, I didn't even have to use my superpowers for this one. She called you John, not Johnny, so I knew she was a business acquaintance. And she looked at me like she wanted to slap my eyeballs out of my head and feed them to me. That's how I knew she'd slept with you."

She lifted her glass in a little salute to him and grinned at his expression. "You grew up with three women, and you didn't realize how astute we are?"

"You're right on that count. How was your dinner?"

"Fabulous. And yours?"

"Delicious, but not as good as your cooking."

Ayanna beamed and excused herself to go freshen up. He rose from the table as she left. After attending to the necessities, she washed her hands and was checking her makeup when the door to the ladies' room opened and in walked Peyton Smith.

"I thought that was you," the other woman said. "I had to see for myself who that drab little thing was with John."

Ayanna sighed deeply. The woman might be a corporate giant, but when it came to common sense, she demonstrated very little. Ayanna obligingly put out her arms and executed a perfect runway spin.

"There you go. If you want to look any closer we'd have to start dating, and you aren't my type." She walked a few steps toward the door and turned back to Peyton with a look of concern on her face. "Look, it's not my business, but you might want to line up the girls because lefty looks like she's about to head for the border."

Peyton turned to the mirror and gasped. Before Ayanna left, she could see her frantically trying to push and shove the unruly blobs back into their corral. She was wearing a true Mona Lisa smile when she reached the lobby where Johnny was waiting.

"Where to now? Dancing, a drive by the river, live music or what? Anything you want, it's yours."

"Then I want a nice drive by the river on our way back to the villa. Then I want to…" She stood on her toes to whisper in his ear.

"We can be there in ten minutes." He grinned as they waited for the valet to bring the car around.

It was more like an hour before they got back to the villa. Despite his teasing, Johnny did take them the long way home. It was the perfect ending to a perfect day. When they got back to the suite, Johnny told her he had a surprise for her.

"It's in the other bedroom. Go in there and see how you like it."

She went into the bedroom and found a short silk nightgown with thin ribbon ties and a matching robe. Both of them were so sheer she could see straight through them, and she couldn't wait to put them on. She took off her clothes and freshened up before donning the ensemble. It was an amazing shade of red, and it looked daring but feminine. She went into the living room expecting to see Johnny waiting for her. There was a trail of rose petals instead. She followed them across the living room and into the other bedroom. The door was open and the petals led into the room, right up to the bed. The covers were turned back, and there were scented candles burning all around.

Johnny was in the bed wearing a smile and red silk boxers. Seductive music was playing and there was a bottle of champagne nestled in a silver ice bucket. A crystal bowl of fresh fruit and a bowl of whipped cream were next to it. She was so surprised that she didn't know what to say.

"Johnny, this is… Wow, you weren't kidding when you said you had a surprise," she murmured.

He was looking at her with deep appreciation. "Stop talking and come here, woman. Walk slowly so I can get a good look at you."

Ayanna blew him a kiss and turned like a model. She held the robe open so he could see what awaited him under its sheer cover, then turned around and slipped it off her shoulders. She looked back at him before letting it flutter to the floor. Executing another slow turn, she finally started walking to the bed with slow, measured steps. She put one knee on the bed and leaned in for a kiss. She licked his lips and gently sucked the tip of his tongue.

"How was that?"

By way of answer, he simply scooped her up and put her on the cushiony softness of the bed. "I don't have any words to describe it. This is going to have to be show-and-tell."

She put her head on the pile of pillows, and he kissed her, slow and deep, while his hands touched her all over. He stroked her sides, her stomach and hips and somehow managed to untie the ribbon straps and take the nightie off her so fast she forgot she'd had it on. He didn't even break the kiss when he took off his boxers. Lying naked next to him was amazing. His skin was hot and smooth, and the feel of his body on hers set her on fire. Her hands stroked his smooth shaven head as he kissed down her chest to her already engorged nipples.

By now his touch was so familiar that her body reacted at once, and she was arching her back as he gently nibbled the ultra-sensitive tips. The nibbling turned into the hard suction she loved, and she could feel an orgasm mounting. He knew she was about to come, and his clever fingers plunged into her so he could bring her closer to the brink. Just when she was about to explode, his tongue replaced his fingers. It was like fireworks bursting all over.

He placed her long legs over his shoulders and continued to lavish her with his lips and tongue until she came again. He wouldn't relent until she had a third soul-shattering climax and her voice was raspy from moaning and calling his name. He finally slowed down and began to lick his way up her body until they were face-to-face. He kissed her, and she sighed with bliss as she tasted herself on his lips and his tongue. She sucked his lower lip and caressed his face with both her hands.

She was trembling, but it wasn't from being cold; it was because of the way he made her feel. He held her tight while she came back to herself. Once her breathing had slowed down he asked if she was thirsty. When she nodded, he gently let her go so he could pour the champagne.

"Told you you'd be loud."

Ayanna pouted and sipped her icy cold drink. "It wasn't my fault. You made me," she said.

"I made you what? Say the words, Ayanna."

She wanted to tell him the truth, which was that he'd made her fall in love with him. Next to her sons and her family, she'd never known love like this, and she didn't know how she was going to do without it. But she took the coward's way out and played along.

"You made me lose my mind along with every inhibition I've ever had. How's that?"

Johnny looked satisfied. "It's a start."

"I've got your start right here, darling. Hand me that bowl of whipped cream," she said.

"Okay, here's the cream. What else?" he asked, looking at the fruit.

"Lie down."

He did so, but with a dubious look on his face. "Don't get scared. This isn't going to hurt a bit. Do you like whipped cream?"

"Yeah, sure, who doesn't like whipped cream?"

Ayanna held the bowl in one hand and dipped her finger into the cream. She licked it off and smiled. "I love whipped cream." She dipped her finger again and held it to his lips. His long tongue licked it off and he ended by sucking her finger, which made a chill go over her, but she ignored it.

"I'll eat anything with whipped cream on it," she

purred. "I'd happily eat mud if it was covered with whipped cream."

She moved closer to Johnny and spooned the cool fluffy cream onto his manhood, which was already hard and ready. She used her fingers to make sure it was evenly distributed. He was watching her with lowered lids, his eyes heavy with desire. She leaned down and began to lick the cream off while her hands were busy stroking him and holding him in place. She could hear him moaning her name over and over, and the moans turned to long groans of extreme pleasure. He had clearly reached a point of no return at the very moment she finished divesting him of all the cream.

She had barely raised her head when he rolled over and grabbed her so fast she couldn't blink. He entered her fast and hard and filled her to the brim with every thrust. Their mouths joined in a long hot kiss that ended only because Johnny had to look into her eyes. This was different than any of the times they'd made love. It was hot, urgent and even more fulfilling than before. Ayanna moved her hips instinctively, and her walls tightened on him. His eyes closed and he thrust once more, even harder, while she used her hips to pump with him until he exploded on a long hoarse cry that was pure passion, but something else, too.

Minutes later they were still tightly wrapped in each other and still locked together because neither one of them wanted to end the embrace. When he was finally able to speak again, Johnny said, "I didn't mean for that to happen. I was going to give you pleasure all night because I didn't want you to be uncomfortable. That was my plan, but it failed miserably."

Ayanna kissed him and rubbed her nose in his goatee. "You gave me more than mere pleasure, darling. That was..." She paused while she tried to think of the right word.

"Yes, it was," he agreed. "It was very, very special. Almost as special as you are."

He kissed her forehead and rolled over so that she was resting on his chest. While she drifted off to sleep, he stared at the box of condoms on the bedside table and wondered what they'd just done. Ayanna moved closer to him and drowsily said his name. He pulled her closer, and he knew it didn't matter. He was in love for the first time in his life, and if he'd just planted his seed in her lovely garden, so much the better.

Chapter 10

Ayanna had three more days of her vacation left. Johnny was pleased to find out that she didn't have to return to work right away because, as he told her, he wanted to monopolize her time. She was a revelation for him; she was gorgeous, no question, but her beauty wasn't her only attraction. He enjoyed her company because she was a good conversationalist and a good listener. She was the sexiest woman he'd ever met, and she did nothing to emphasize it other than be herself.

She didn't load herself up with heavy perfumes, she didn't drape herself in gaudy jewelry and she didn't dress like a hooker. But she always looked perfect to him, whether she was dressed for church or a night on the town. Even in jeans, like she was now, she was the cutest thing he'd ever seen. They were on their way back to Illinois from Charleston and she was reading aloud from one of her romance novels, but it wasn't holding his attention. Now that he knew the kind of heat she was packing in her slender body, other people's sex lives were of no interest to him, especially the lives that were only on paper.

He reached over and took the book from her fingertips, smiling when she laughed.

"Getting bored or heated up?" she asked playfully.

"Neither one," he said. "I'm thinking about what we're going to do for the next five days. You have three more days of vacation plus a weekend. What would you like to do?"

"Laundry, for sure. Sort the boys' clothes so I can figure out what they'll need for school this fall. Maybe paint the kitchen."

"You are the most conscientious woman I've ever met, but you need to learn how to play," Johnny chided her.

"I do know how to play," Ayanna protested.

"No, you don't. We're talking about five days where you don't have to go into the office and all you can think of to fill the time is more work. Loosen up, Ayanna! You're too young to be so serious."

"It's easy to be carefree when you don't have kids," Ayanna pointed out. "I have a lot of responsibilities. How are things going to get done if I don't do them?"

She sounded defensive and a little hurt, which were the last things Johnny wanted to make her feel. He took her hand and kissed the back of it.

"I'm sorry, sweetheart, I wasn't trying to make fun of you, and I certainly didn't want to belittle you in any way. You're an amazing person, and you have all my respect. But," he said, kissing her hand again, "I want you to have more relaxation in your life. From what I can see, you work hard, and I just want you to play a little, too."

He smiled when she returned the kiss. Her soft lips felt wonderful on his hand. "So you think I need a little more playtime, hmm?"

"Yep. And I'll be more than willing to be your playdate. Starting tonight," he said with a grin.

"I hate it when you smile like that," Ayanna said. "When you do that you look so darned good I can't refuse you anything."

Johnny laughed so hard he almost missed their exit. "Does that mean I get my way?"

"Yes, it does. You win," she said with a sigh.

"Oh no, angel, we win. Both of us," he reminded her.

Ayanna couldn't believe her audacious idea even while she was conceiving it. A few weeks ago this would have been completely out of the question, but through Johnny, she'd discovered a new side of her womanhood. She'd finally gotten in touch with her inner diva, the femme fatale sexy siren that she'd ignored for years. Now that Johnny had let the genie out of the bottle she wasn't trying to put it back in. She was, in fact, trying to find more and better ways of expressing herself, and tonight she was going to show

Johnny that not only did she know how to have fun, but she knew how to play, too.

He'd gone into his office in the morning, and she'd talked to him a couple of times on the phone. She'd invited him over for dinner, asking him what his favorite dish was.

"Whatever you cook. I'm not picky, and whatever you make tastes good," he'd said.

Since it was a really warm day and she didn't want to heat up the house, she decided to grill a chicken and rosemary skewered potatoes and keep them warm in the oven. With the chicken she would serve ratatouille, a green salad and her homemade lemon squares for dessert. She had to time everything perfectly so that the meal would be ready when Johnny got there and that she would be ready, too.

She took a long hot shower and scrubbed away every trace of charcoal smoke from grilling the chicken. She shampooed her hair three times to make sure that its only scent would be sweet and floral, not smoky. She used her precious stash of Chanel No. 5 body cream from head to toe, and then applied her makeup. It was a little heavier than she usually wore it; she actually hadn't worn makeup as heavy since the last time she'd danced in public with Todd. But she still knew how to work it.

Foundation, blush a shade darker than usual and charcoal eye shadow that deepened and lengthened her eyes. Gold highlighter and inky-black liquid liner made her look much more glam than usual. Several coats of black mascara made her lashes look so long and lush they appeared to be false, and she was satisfied that she looked nothing like her normal self. She combed setting gel through her hair and parted it on one side, slicking it back. Adding a little gold highlight powder to her collarbone and her cleavage, she added a mist of Chanel eau de parfum and began to get dressed. Johnny was due in fifteen minutes, and she knew he'd be prompt.

Sure enough, he arrived right on time, and he'd brought her flowers, a beautiful bouquet of irises, freesia, calla lilies and roses. And in the other hand he had a giant houseplant. "Johnny, you're so thoughtful. Why two?"

"Because I know you like flowers. And I know you like plants, so why shouldn't you have both?" He put the plant on the coffee table and handed her the flowers. He leaned in for a kiss, and she turned her cheek. He kissed it, and then stood back and looked at her.

"Are we going out tonight? You look way better than I do," he said.

It was true; he was wearing a short-sleeved print rayon shirt and jeans, and Ayanna was wearing a black pinstriped three-piece pant suit. The vest was buttoned up, and she had on a white blouse with the collar turned up. Her lips were sexy but looked unfamiliar with the shiny deep red gloss she had on.

She put the flowers on the dining room table and walked toward Johnny with a look that meant business on her pretty face. When she reached him, she pulled his head down to hers, and instead of kissing him, she ran her mint-tasting tongue over his lips. "Sit down," she whispered in his ear.

He held up both hands and did exactly as she asked, backing up until he was on the sofa. He crossed his legs and spread his arms out across the back of the couch. He watched wordlessly as Ayanna put on a black fedora and turned her back to him. She used the remote control to start the music. A long blues riff filled the room as "Loan Me a Dime" by the legendary Boz Scaggs came on. Ayanna dropped the remote like it was red-hot, sliding her legs apart and bending her knees until her butt touched the floor before taking a stance that showed off her long legs, made even longer by the four-inch stiletto pumps she was wearing.

The song was slow and lush, and Ayanna matched her movements to every beat. First her jacket came off, slowly, but with such deliberate finesse that it was like an act of foreplay. She slowly turned to face Johnny and began to unbutton her vest with excruciating precision until it was finally open. She slid it off and tossed it across the room to Johnny, who caught it with one hand.

The dance went on, a slow, sensual exhibition that was both erotic and artistic. She could hear Johnny groan as her wide-leg pants were eased down her legs revealing lace-topped hose attached to black garters. She stepped out of the pants without missing a beat and finally started taking off her blouse. It had French cuffs, and she prolonged her striptease by taking off the cuff links one at a time before beginning on the buttons. When they were all undone, she pulled the blouse open to reveal a black-lace merry widow that made the most of her small rounded breasts and made her waist look incredibly tiny.

She tossed the blouse into the air, and as it fluttered down, she executed some moves with her hips that could have caused a riot in a gentleman's ballet. All that was missing was a pole, but Johnny didn't seem to mind.

The song was thirteen minutes and three seconds long, but Johnny didn't seem terribly interested in hearing the end of it. Before she could finish the dance and toss her fedora at him, he had left the sofa and picked her up as he kissed every bit of the shiny black cherry gloss off her mouth. She had to wrap her arms around his neck and her legs around his waist to steady them.

"I wasn't finished," she murmured.

"We can finish in the bedroom," he groaned.

"But the chicken will dry out," she whispered.

"That's why God made gravy," he informed her as he took her to the only place he wanted her right then—the bed.

They finally managed to eat dinner after their appetite for each other was satisfied. The chicken and potatoes weren't dried out, as Ayanna feared. Johnny was wearing a towel and nothing else, and Ayanna had on a little Japanese kimono with nothing underneath. She sat in his lap, and they fed each other with their fingers and talked. "Ayanna, you're full of surprises. I love that in you," he said as he nuzzled her neck.

"I told you I could play," she murmured.

"You're right. I'm never going to challenge you again."

He ate another bite from her fingers and sighed in repletion. "You should be running a five-star restaurant," he said. "Why aren't you doing that instead of working for a construction company?"

Ayanna shrugged. "I never went to the Cordon Bleu like I'd planned. I needed to work, and I needed a stable job with benefits that would give me time with the boys. Restaurant work is long and hard and you work crazy hours. The benefits suck if there are any at all. So I started teaching. I loved it, but it's not the best money in the world. Why do they pay professional athletes so much and teachers so little?" she mused.

"I have no idea. It's a screwed up system, I'll grant you. So why did you quit teaching?"

"Two reasons. It was too hard to make a nine-month income stretch to twelve months for one thing. For another, there were going to be layoffs in my district. Since I didn't have as much seniority as some of the other teachers, I knew my head would be on the block. Then I heard about the job with Hunter Construction. Nick was paying more than I was making, the hours were about the same and I'd have weekends and holidays off. I don't get the summers off anymore, but the money makes it easier for us," she said.

"But what about when the boys go to college? Cameron will be gone in a couple of years, and Alec will be right behind him because he's in that accelerated program. What about picking up your dream where you left off?"

Ayanna looked at him in surprise. "How did you know Alec was in an accelerated program?"

Johnny gave her a smug smile. "I know because he told me. Alec and Cameron and I have gotten to be quite close, thank you. I know more than you think. You've raised a couple of really wonderful young men, Ayanna."

"I think we raised each other," she confessed. "They're really good kids, and they haven't given me any grief. They're pretty well-behaved and cooperative. I keep waiting for horns to sprout and police to show up at my door, but praise God, nothing like that has happened. I tried to raise them like my parents raised us, and so far it's worked. I'm waiting for those teenage hormones to kick in, though. I've heard some horror stories from my friends about adolescence."

"If they haven't started acting out yet, maybe they won't. I was a hellion when I was little, but I was real mellow as a teenager. I was too scared of my dad to act out," he said, and laughed.

"Yes, but they don't have a dad," Ayanna said and could have cheerfully bitten her tongue off for saying it. It sounded like she was asking for something from Johnny that she knew she wasn't going to get. Her phone rang, and she flew off his lap to answer it.

"Cameron! I was just talking about you and Alec. How are you guys?" She had to turn away from Johnny because the sight of him nude from the waist up sitting at the kitchen table was just too much for her to take. There was only so much heat one woman could handle.

Chapter 11

Ayanna had such a good time with Johnny that she didn't even mind the inquisition when her vacation was officially over. She knew that Billie and Dakota would want all the dish, and she wasn't about to begrudge them. A week after they returned to Chicago, she went over to Dakota's house for a girls' night. Along with Toni Beauchamp, Dakota's best friend, they were gathered in Dakota's kitchen around the table. They had coffee and peach ice cream with Billie's delicious peach cobbler. Ayanna was praising it when Billie held up her hand.

"Okay, you can stop with the false modesty. I've always been known as the baker in the family but my big brother let me know that mine doesn't hold a candle to yours. I swear, every bite he puts in his mouth these days is followed by him saying 'Ayanna's is better,' or 'Ayanna does hers different.' You've got him spoiled rotten already," she said.

Ayanna blushed pink, but the other women wouldn't let her get away with it. Dakota and Toni laughed at Billie's statement, but they assured Ayanna that it was a good thing.

"Honey, if that man thinks you can do something in the kitchen no other woman can, let him!" Dakota said.

Toni agreed wholeheartedly. "I don't do a lot of cooking, but I am like the sandwich queen. I can make sandwiches that will make you cry, they're so good. Zane won't eat anyone else's now," she said. "Of course, that means I have to pack him a gourmet lunch to take to work every day, but it's a small price to pay."

Ayanna looked around the table at the three women, all of whom had been married less than two years. They were acting like she would soon be joining their ranks, and she felt like a faker. And a failure. It wasn't going to happen for her.

"So, you and Johnny went to Columbia to drop off the boys, and you stayed two days." Dakota, the investigative reporter, always liked to get her facts lined up. "What was your favorite part of your visit home?"

Ayanna's eyes crinkled in a smile. "Going to the drugstore!" They all looked puzzled until she explained. "My ex-fiancé was going to medical school, but he ended up being a pharmacist because he's terrified of the sight of blood. Anyway, I had to get Alec's allergy prescription filled, and we went to pick it up," she began. The story was short but hilarious.

They went to the Walgreens drugstore that was closest to her mother's house in the University Hill section of town. While they were there, Ayanna started walking the aisles to see if there was anything she needed. She loved drugstores and was always inspecting the end caps where the clearance items were displayed. Johnny was walking behind her when she stopped, her eyes caught by something on the shelf.

"Johnny, what is that?"

He'd picked up the item and told her it was a personal lubricant. "I don't think you need that, but if you want to try some, go ahead."

Ayanna had blushed bright red, and Johnny's arms had gone around her at once. "Look, sweetness, I can promise you that we're not going to need anything but each other. But there's nothing wrong with using creams and oils or gels or whatever turns you on."

He had rubbed his cheek against her hair while she stared at the amazing array of goods. "Cherry-flavored, raspberry-chocolate, mint... My goodness there's a lot of stuff here." She leaned against Johnny and smiled. "But all I want is you. There can't be anything on those shelves that could make me feel better than you do."

He answered her with a lingering kiss. "There is one thing I need, though." He reached for two boxes of condoms. The PA announced that her prescription was ready, and they went to the back of the store to claim it. Johnny put the two boxes of condoms on the counter and pulled out his credit card to pay for everything. Ayanna was looking at the store's weekly circular when she heard her name.

"Ayanna? Ayanna Porter?"

She turned to see Percy Stubbins behind the pharmacist's counter. "Percy! Fancy meeting you here."

"It's been a long time, Ayanna. Are you moving back here or something?"

"No, I just brought my sons to spend the summer with my mom." Percy was staring at her so hard she thought he'd developed X-ray vision along with the receded hairline, jowls and paunch he was sporting.

"Do we need anything else, or is this it, sweetness?"

Percy had looked from Ayanna to Johnny and back again. There was Johnny, all six foot four inches of him in a short-sleeved polo shirt that showed off his magnificent biceps and jeans that made his long, hard legs look even better than usual. He'd put his hand on Ayanna's back, which was bared in a sexy little sundress, and the gesture wasn't missed by anyone within ten feet of the couple. It was a simple gesture that signified affection and possession in equal parts.

Ayanna looked up at Johnny with a secret smile that made Percy drop his ink pen. "I think that's all."

Percy's glasses actually fogged up when Johnny kissed Ayanna like there was no one else around. He cleared his throat loudly and began to ring up the prescription, and when he saw the two boxes of condoms, his light brown face reddened, and his grandpa-looking eyeglasses slipped.

"Magnums!" The word was out before he realized he'd spoken aloud.

While he was fumbling to put their purchases in a bag, Ayanna asked about his wife.

"She's fat, um, fine," Percy said. "So is this your, um…"

"My manners, what must you think of me? Percy Stubbins, this is John Phillips. John, this is Percy."

Percy nodded and tried to say something suave. "So are you two, um, ah, married?"

Johnny bent down for another kiss. "Not yet. Nice meeting you."

When she finished telling the story, minus the condom part and the marriage comment, Toni was laughing so hard that tears were running down her face, and Dakota was looking at Ayanna with new respect. Billie was, too. Ayanna looked from one sister to the other.

"What?"

"This is a first, honey. Johnny doesn't do the domestic thing at all. I can't ever remember him doing normal, mundane things with a woman. Certainly not driving fourteen hours with her and her kids, not meeting her family and going to the neighborhood drugstore. Never!" Billie shook her head in amazement while she drank a glass of milk, her new favorite beverage since becoming pregnant.

"Yes, but—"

"Take that word out of your vocabulary, honey. Your life is getting ready to change, big time," Dakota said wisely. A soft cry from the baby monitor caused her to excuse herself and go see about little Bethany.

Dakota had sounded so much like Johnny when she said that. "Take that word out of your vocabulary." They'd said the same thing to tell her to stop saying "but". In the world of these women, there were no buts. Nothing stood in their way, nothing was impossible for them. A chirp from the baby monitor made Toni get to her feet.

"I'd better go see about the big guy," she said with a smile. Her baby was a few months older than Bethany, and he was asleep in the nursery with her— or at least he had been.

Billie waited until she and Ayanna were alone. "What's on your mind, girl? I can tell something is bothering you. Has Johnny done his famous disappearing act?"

"Oh no," Ayanna said. "I talk to him every day. Twice a day, usually. And we had dinner last night. He wanted to have dinner tonight, but I had plans. He's cooking dinner for me tomorrow night at his place."

"Nick's old apartment? Have you seen it yet?" When Ayanna said no, Billie grinned. "Wait until you check the place out! Dakota called it a pimp's pleasure palace, but I loved it. It's wild." She finished her milk and went to the sink to rinse out the glass.

"But so much for Nick's old place, you'll see it tomorrow. What's up, Ayanna?"

Ayanna knew Billie too well to try and bluff her, but she didn't want to put all her business out in the street, either. "Pre-period blues is all. You know how I am. I walk around sniveling for a few days every month."

"Dakota was the same way. I think having the baby mellowed out her hormones, though. She doesn't seem to have that problem anymore."

The conversation switched easily to other topics, and when Dakota and Toni returned with the babies on their shoulders, Ayanna felt like she'd dodged a high-caliber bullet. There were a few more questions about her vacation, but luckily Nick walked into the house followed by Jason and then Toni's husband Zane and all personal inquiries ceased.

Ayanna felt oddly lonely as she drove home. There was so much love and caring among the three couples she'd just left that she felt left out. She'd cared strongly for Percy at one time. She certainly thought she loved him enough to marry him. But when her sister was killed, the bottom dropped out of her world. She didn't even consider not taking Alec and Cameron, because she loved them dearly and because it was her sister's wish. The guardianship had been in place for years, even though she never thought she'd be called upon to follow through with it.

Percy wanted nothing to do with Alec and Cameron and made her choose between him and her nephews. Without a second's hesitation, she told him to take a flying leap. Her mother told her then that he was all wrong for her.

"Ayanna, any man who could impose a condition like that on you isn't worth your time or your tears.

There's someone waiting for you, and when you meet him, you'll know. He'll treat you like a queen, and those boys will be his princes. Just give it time, and he'll find you."

Ayanna parked in the garage and went into the house, dutifully turning off the alarm before checking all the windows and doors. It was still early, barely nine, and it was still light out. She looked around for something to do, but the house was spotless, and there wasn't even a load of laundry waiting its turn. She decided to take a shower and go to bed early, with her latest romance. She wanted to call Johnny, but she wasn't going to wear out his number. They had talked earlier, and he knew she was doing girls' night with his sisters and Toni. It was good to have space, she mused. There was nothing worse than being a clingy woman who couldn't spend a night alone.

When she got out of the shower, her phone was ringing. The caller ID showed her mother's number, and she answered at once. "Hello?"

"Hi, Ma! How was your girls' night?"

"It was fun, Cameron. And how did you know what my plans were for the evening?"

Alec's voice answered her. "John told us."

Her eyebrows went up in surprise. "You talked to John?"

"Sure, we talk every day. He e-mails us, and we e-mail him back. We send him cartoons."

Ayanna rallied from her shock ,and they enjoyed a nice conversation. She was still amazed after she hung up the phone. She talked to the boys every day and to John every day and she just found out that they had been communicating with each other all along. She knew they had a mutual admiration society going on, but this was really touching.

She was putting on lotion when the phone rang again. This time it was John.

"Wanna go to the movies?"

"Hello to you, too. It's kind of late for the movies, isn't it?"

"Yes, if we were going to a theater. But if I brought the popcorn and the movie, we could watch one at home. Is it too late for that?"

"That sounds nice."

"See you in thirty minutes."

Johnny was prompt, as always. Ayanna couldn't really decide if she liked him better in casual clothes or dress clothes, because he looked so good in both styles. He was very casual tonight in a football jersey and jeans with athletic shoes. She wasn't dressed up, either, in a red tank top, denim shorts and bare feet.

After a brief kiss, they went into the living room, and he showed her the bag from the rental store. "No, just surprise me," she said. "You get it queued up, and I'll pop the popcorn."

She came back into the living room with a big bowl and a stack of napkins. "I have to go get the sodas, and I'll be right back."

Johnny insisted on getting the drinks. He brought

them in, sat next to her on the sofa and put his arm around her shoulders. "Ready?"

He pressed the play button and Tyler Perry's *Why Did I Get Married?* came on.

"That's a surprising choice," she said.

"You don't like Tyler Perry?"

"I love him, but this is dangerously close to a chick flick," she warned.

"I'll take my chances." He kissed her again. "No talking."

She curled up next to him and settled back to watch the movie. Somewhere between the opening credits and the end of the movie, she drifted off to sleep. She woke up from the kisses he was planting all over her face.

"Wake up, sweetness. You need to go to bed because tomorrow morning is going to come all too early."

She smiled sleepily. "Why don't you spend the night?"

"Because neither one of us will get any sleep. Tomorrow is Friday, you're coming over and I get to show off my skills and have my way with you. Plus, nobody has to get up early on Saturday. That's a better plan for us both. Come walk me to the door, and turn on the alarm."

Protesting, she yawned her way off the sofa and automatically reached for the popcorn bowl and glasses, which were gone.

"My mama raised me right," he said. "I took care of them."

Their good-night kiss was sweet but much too short for Ayanna. Johnny was adamant that she get her rest, though, and he left, but she suddenly didn't feel alone. She felt cherished, which was ridiculous. She touched her lips and thought about him calling her boys every day. Maybe theirs was just a friendship with summer benefits, but it was wonderful while it lasted.

Chapter 12

Ayanna looked over the art deco style apartment building. It looked pretty normal to her eyes. Billie had told her that the place was something else, but she couldn't see it. The lobby was stylish and understated and the workmanship was outstanding. She took the elevator up to Johnny's floor and looked down the hallway. He was standing in the doorway waiting for her, which was endearing for some reason.

"Welcome to my crib," he said in a gangsta voice. He ushered her in the door and waited for her reaction.

"Oh my. This is something, isn't it?"

It was wild, just like Billie said. There was the longest couch she'd ever seen, done in camel-colored leather with cheetah spots hand-painted on it. The chairs were obnoxious but entertaining. They were gold velvet high heels. There were many cheap versions of the chair available at any bargain furniture mart, but these were the original art-gallery versions. The floors were beautiful hardwood, but there was a horrible area rug in bright peacock-blue with faux zebra stripes. Ayanna was stunned.

"Well, at least the rug matches the walls," she said lamely. It was true; the walls were covered in the same shade of blue. Raw silk, the carpet was obviously expensive, but the color was blinding. The lights were blinding, too. They were big pillars of rough cut glass that were way too bright. "The Flintstones called. They want their lamps back."

She stared at the huge heavy glass dining-room table and the hideous chairs. They were made out of cowhide or pony skin or something. They were hairy, and each one was painted to resemble some poor wild animal. Just awful. She glanced at the huge light fixture over the table and groaned. "I always thought Nick had such good taste," she murmured.

Johnny laughed. "He does now. Dakota got him on the right path. He was with this woman who called herself a decorator, and he just let her have at it. We like to tease him about this place. Come on in the kitchen, it's safe. You look great, by the way. And you smell fantastic."

She was wearing a black wrap dress with big red flowers on it that came from the clearance rack at T.J. Maxx. This was the first time she'd worn it since last summer, and she was glad it still looked good. She was also wearing red sandals from the same place. She smelled wonderful, too, because she'd found a bottle of Safari in the bath and body department. She denied herself perfume and jewelry because she watched her budget so carefully. Her mother always hooked her up on her birthday and Christmas, but she used the fragrances very sparingly to make them last. She was pleased that Johnny noticed because she had done it for him.

She smiled to herself as she followed him into the surprisingly nice kitchen. There was nothing weird in here; it was super clean with gleaming appliances and a marble-topped work island in the middle of the room.

"This is much better. What smells so good?"

"Another surprise," he said mysteriously. "It'll be ready in a few if you want to do whatever it is you women do before you eat."

"I do this," she said, pulling him down for a kiss. "Now, where's the bathroom so I can perform my secret lady ritual?"

He showed her the bathroom, and once again she was impressed. "This I like." It was a soft buff color, all marble with gold fixtures. The tub was almost as big as the one at the Wild Dunes Resort and was outfitted with whirlpool jets and dual faucets with handheld showerheads. The tub was enclosed in glass, and there were glass shelves that held some really luxurious-looking towels.

"Yeah, that gives me some ideas. I've got to start

looking for a house next week. Good thing I've got a
brother-in-law in the business."

He left to check on dinner, and she washed her hands
while admiring the pedestal sink. She wondered what
kind of house he'd want. Jason was the leading real-
estate mogul in the city, so he'd certainly have the
inside track on the best property available. What would
his bachelor pad look like? *Probably not like this one,
except for the bathroom.* She was still smiling when she
went back to the kitchen.

"What can I do to help?"

Johnny was doing something mysterious at the
stove. "Not a thing except go into the living room and
sit down on the sofa. We're eating in there tonight."

She went down the hall and did as he asked. Now
that the initial shock of the decor had worn off, she
noticed two low tables next to the sofa. There was a
tablecloth on one table with big cloth napkins, but no
silverware. There were big thick goblets and a flat bowl
with a single flower floating in water over some glass
pebbles. Johnny came in the room with a huge covered
tray, which he put on the other table.

The music was already playing, and it was perfect
for the occasion, low and sultry jazz. Johnny grinned
at her. "I've really got you thinking now, don't I? We're
going to sit on the floor," he said, indicating four big
silk-covered cushions. "I want you to sit here, and I'll
sit here." Once she was comfortably ensconced on her
cushions, he told her there was one last thing he had to
do. "Don't get nervous," he added.

He turned off the lights, and the room was completely dark. So dark that she couldn't see a thing, not even the streetlights, because he'd closed the blinds and drawn the curtains. "What happened?"

She was relieved to feel his hand on her arm. "I said don't get nervous," he reminded her. "I heard about this restaurant where they turn off the lights completely and all the servers are blind. It's supposed to really enhance the dining experience. Are you game?"

Ayanna nodded her head and then laughed because she realized in a split second that he couldn't see her. "Yes, let's go for it. What happens now?"

"First I want you to take a deep breath and tell me what you smell," he said.

He was holding her hand, and the warmth was comforting and stimulating at the same time. Coming out of the pitch black of the room, his voice sounded even deeper and sexier than it normally did.

"I smell that flower, the one on the table. It smells like spring, sweet and light. I smell basil, rosemary and pepper," she told him.

"Very good. I'm going to let go of your hand for a moment, okay?"

In seconds he was pressing a goblet into her hands. "Okay, smell that. What does it smell like?"

She inhaled the contents of the glass and smiled. "It's wine. I smell raspberries and black cherries and, mmm, lavender, I think."

"Very good. Taste it," he said.

She took a sip and the flavors rolled across her

tongue and warmed the back of her throat. "This is very good," she praised. "I really like it." She took another sip, and he reached over to take the goblet from her hands.

"Everything we're eating is finger food," he said. He reached over and somehow found her face with no effort. "Open your mouth, baby."

She did and was rewarded with a bite of the tenderest filet she'd ever tasted. It was marinated in the herbs she'd named as well as the wine she'd just tasted. It was just the beginning of a wonderful meal. He'd made steamed snow peas, marinated cucumbers, the filet mignon and bacon-wrapped bites of chicken. It was a long and sensual meal and her senses were so heightened by everything that she thought she could hear their hearts beating. She felt so close to him she could have sworn they were breathing in unison.

Dessert was being served in the bedroom. He wouldn't tell her what it was, and he made her close her eyes while he led her to the room so the spell of darkness wouldn't be broken. Once they were in the bedroom, he undressed her and put her in the middle of the bed. "Don't move," he cautioned. "This bed is kind of different."

When he was naked and sitting behind her, she relaxed into his arms. He kissed the back of her neck and she shivered in anticipation. "What are we having?"

"You're having chocolate-covered strawberries. And I'm having you with whipped cream," he said while he caressed her breasts.

"I told you I love whipped cream," she reminded him.

"I know you do, and so do I. And I'm going to enjoy every bit of you."

He lay her back on the bed and parted her legs gently, helped her bend her knees. When she was positioned to his liking, she had to bite her lips to stifle a gasp when she felt the cool cream between her legs.

"What goes around comes around, sweetness. Open wide," he growled.

The next morning Ayanna drifted slowly into wakefulness. She didn't want to move because she felt so relaxed and well-loved. The things Johnny had done to her last night belonged in the pages of a book of erotica. She laughed to herself as she remembered every single moment of their lovemaking. Everything had been done in the pitch blackness of the apartment, which made everything seem so much more intense. They even took a shower in the dark, and she knew she'd never look at a handheld showerhead the same way again.

She rolled over on the silky sheets and found Johnny's warm body next to hers. This time he hadn't gone out for food and coffee or anything; he was right next to her where she wanted him to be. His arms went around her automatically, and he held her tight. She'd gotten so used to doing things by touch and not sight that she was reluctant to open her eyes. She had to force them open slowly, and when she did, she was stunned to see red satin sheets. And they were on a round bed, no less. *This is just like my dream,* she thought. *The hot dream I had the night of Billie's house-warming when I dreamed about a beautiful bald man and some red sheets. Snap!*

Determined not to let him catch her with morning mouth, she slipped out of bed and looked in her big purse for her toothbrush. After brushing her teeth thoroughly and doing a few other necessary morning things, she went into the kitchen to see what she could make for breakfast. The calendar on the refrigerator door caught her eye. She kept staring at the date, trying to make it register. Something was supposed to happen on the fifteenth. What was it?

Shrugging, she opened the refrigerator and took out a carton of eggs. Her hands started shaking as it came to her in a rush. Her period should have started three days ago. Where was it?

Chapter 13

Ayanna was trying her best not to dissolve into a pool of panic. It was a week since the erotically sexy dinner at Johnny's, and her period was still nowhere to be found. They had gone without a condom only once— that night in Isle of Palms. Surely one little slip couldn't have left her with child. She wasn't going to give energy to the thought. It wasn't unheard of for her to skip a period. They would come like clockwork every single month on the same day. Then the cycle would change by about five days, and it would start coming on *that* day for about a year before skipping to another day. That had to be it; her body was changing its date cycle for reasons known only to it.

She did her best to hide any sign of angst from

Johnny. They were too busy having a good time for her to derail their train with a late period. It would turn out to be nothing so there was no reason for her to rock the boat. In the meantime, she was enjoying every moment she was with him. He could always think of something exciting to do, and even when they weren't out and about, he was the best company she could imagine.

They went to the legendary Taste of Chicago and walked around sampling so many different restaurant offerings that even Johnny got full. They went to two Cubs games, to the movies and they did things with his sisters and their husbands. They went out dancing often because he said he loved to see her move. He was by far the most thoughtful man she'd ever known, and her love for him grew every day.

One evening she finally talked to him about his relationship with Alec and Cameron. They were sitting on the small screened porch she had added to the house when she bought it.

"By the way, the boys told me that you talk to them and e-mail them," she said. "I was surprised to hear that."

"Why? Do you not want me to? I apologize if I overstepped my bounds or something, but they're such great kids I wanted to make sure they were having a good time. And I won't lie to you. I'm trying to make a good impression on their mother. I want her to know that I'll be good to her kids because I like them, not just because I'm crazy about her," he said.

Her eyes filled with tears, and her chin trembled

with the effort not to cry. He was alarmed by her
reaction. He took her hands and led her into the house.
"I don't want your neighbors to think I'm beating you
or something. What's wrong, baby?"

"Nothing's wrong, nothing, nothing. You're just so
sweet and kind and wonderful. I don't know what I've
done to deserve you."

He took her into the living room and sat down on the
sofa with her in his lap. Kissing her teary eyes, he assured
her that she was the wonderful one. "In my entire life, I've
never done anything to deserve you, Ayanna. You are the
most giving, the most incredible person I know. You give
so much and expect so little," he said, kissing her again.

"In fact, I have something for you. I bought it in
Charleston and was keeping it for a surprise. I hope you
like it," he said, pulling a small box out of his pocket.

"It" was the most stunning piece of jewelry she'd
ever seen. A pair of diamond and pearl earrings set in
yellow gold. The iridescent pearls dangled from a ball
of sparkling brown stones, and they were by far the
most incredible things she'd ever seen. "Johnny, these
are amazing," she whispered.

He kissed her before responding. "I'm glad you like
them. Those are chocolate pearls and chocolate diamonds. Try them on. I want to see them against your
skin."

"Diamonds and pearls? You mean they're real?"

"Of course they're real. Do you think I'd give you
fake jewelry? Put them on, Ayanna. I want you to see
how gorgeous they'll look on you."

But she snapped the box shut and handed it back to him. "I can't take these, Johnny. This is way too much. I can't let you spend that kind of money on me."

Johnny sat back and looked at her incredulously. "What do you mean you can't take them? It's just a little gift. It's not like I'm trying to give you the Hope Diamond or something. Can't I show you how I feel about you with a present?"

She was feeling distinctly uncomfortable and got up from his lap. He was so confused by her attitude that he let her. She walked away from him and turned her back, trying to control her hands, which were shaking. Turning to face him she said, "Look, Johnny, if this was a real relationship, sure. But this is a summer fling for us, and we both know it. It's not right for you to spend so much money on me when we're going to go our separate ways in a few weeks."

Johnny rose to his full height. "Summer fling? Who's having a summer fling? I sure as hell am not. All I think about is you, Ayanna, you and Alec and Cameron. All I want is you. I never said anything, but when we made love without the condom I was happy because I thought you might get pregnant and nothing would have made me happier than giving you my child. Does that sound like a summer affair to you?"

"No, it sounds like selfishness," she said with her hands on her hips. "If that's what you wanted, you should be thrilled because my period is over two weeks late! I have two sons, Johnny, two impressionable boys! It's hard enough being a single mother to two boys.

How the hell am I supposed to take care of a third? We barely make ends meet as it is. And you'd be glad to plant another one in me? Thanks a lot!"

Johnny was pacing around her like an angry panther. Her words didn't seem to register with him. He was too furious for that. "So this has been all about sex with you? You were trying to make up for eleven years of celibacy with the first man who came along, is that it? Damn, Ayanna, I thought I was the master of the game, but you got me beat for sure. And I was fool enough to fall in love with you." He stopped pacing and laughed, a harsh bark that held no amusement whatsoever.

"Thanks for a good time. And let me know if you're pregnant. That's all I want to hear from you from now on. E-mail me because I don't want to hear your voice again."

Without another word, he turned and left the house. Ayanna sank into the sofa that still bore his scent and wept. She hadn't cried like this since her sister died, which seemed appropriate because a part of her had just stopped living.

Ayanna spent the next two weeks in total misery. She tried to disguise her feelings, but it was difficult. No, it was impossible, because Billie knew without being told that something was wrong. She came into the office the morning after the horrible argument, and when she saw Ayanna's face, she could tell something disastrous had happened.

"Whatever you're working on can wait. Come on in my office, and tell me what's wrong."

Ayanna turned to her computer and brought up a posting for a property the firm had just acquired. "It's nothing, Billie. I'm just not feeling too well. I miss Alec and Cameron," she said lamely.

"Ayanna, you don't want to cross a cranky pregnant woman. Come with me and unburden yourself or I'll make a huge ugly scene right here in reception," Billie vowed.

Ayanna had to laugh, seeing as how Nick and everyone else was out in the field and there was no one in the office but the two of them. She allowed Billie to usher her into her private office, and the two women sat on the small sofa.

"I know I'm nosy, but you already knew that. You and Johnny were getting along so well. What happened? This is about Johnny, isn't it?" Her eyes were warm with concern.

"We had an argument. A big nasty one," Ayanna admitted. "He thinks I'm only interested in the, um, physical aspects of our relationship, and he says he wants more."

Billie's mouth dropped open. "He asked you to *marry* him?"

"No, no, no! But he said he wanted me to have his child, and he said he loves me," she murmured, unable to meet Billie's eyes.

Billie wasn't looking at Ayanna at the moment; she was digging through her tote bag for something to eat. "That's not like the Johnny I know and love. He's always been a playa," she said between bites of a banana. "I've never known him to stay in a relationship long enough to get really attached. I've never known him to have a relationship, really. You were the first real girlfriend I can ever recall," she said.

"I mean, babies and love are words that are just not in his vocabulary. He must have some really deep feelings for you to even let the words out of his mouth."

"Is this supposed to be making me feel better? Because it's not," Ayanna said sadly.

"I'm sorry, sweetie, I'm just having a hard time getting my head around this. You two were doing so well. What started the argument?"

Ayanna tried to explain and ended up making a muddle out of it. "Billie, he gave me these really expensive earrings, and I told him I couldn't accept them and then things just went all crazy."

"Why couldn't you take them? What's wrong with him giving you a gift?" Billie looked baffled.

"Billie, these earrings were real diamonds and pearls! How could I take something like that from someone who was just having a summer thing with me? I *couldn't*," she answered her own question. "I couldn't let him spend that kind of money on me. It's not like we were really involved," she added.

Billie's expression changed. "You thought he wasn't really interested in something long-lasting and permanent, and you were guarding your heart. Oh, sweetie, I wished I'd known. I could have told you that he was really serious about you. Why wouldn't he be?"

"Why *would* he be? I'm not like you and Dakota and Toni or even your sisters-in-law," she began.

"Thank God you're not like Nip and Tuck." Billie shuddered. "Why on earth would you want to be?"

"Because they're doctors," Ayanna said. "From what I can see, Johnny is used to high-profile career women with titles and degrees and credentials. I'm your basic soccer mom. I have a bachelor's degree and a culinary certificate and two growing boys who can eat me out of house and home. I'm not the type he'd go for long-term so I took what I could get."

Billie put down her banana and stared at Ayanna. "Girl, if you weren't my best friend I'd smack you. Now I'll admit that Johnny has had a tendency to be as shallow as a puddle on a hot day when it comes to women, but I think—no, I *know*—that he was serious about you. He's a good man, despite his playboy ways. One thing I know for sure is that someone's profession or education is the last thing he'd be worried about if he loved the woman. And my question to you is why would you settle for sex anyway? Don't you want to have real love with marriage and babies and all the rest of it? Why the hell are you selling yourself short?"

"Because my first obligation is to my sons," Ayanna said hotly. "They're my true loves and my respon-sibility for life. I'm not going to choose between my boys and a man. They deserve the best mother they can have, and I intend to be that person for them. I'm not going to choose, Billie."

"Question: who asked you to? That jerk of an ex-fiancé told you to choose, and you made the right choice. But has Johnny ever acted as though Alec and Cameron were in the way, or were an inconvenience or a potential burden?"

"No, he didn't," Ayanna said softly.

"No, he didn't, because he's crazy about those boys. And you waited until they were gone for the summer and decided to have a good time with Johnny because it was convenient. Is that what I'm hearing? If that's the case, I can't really blame Johnny for being angry. He thought you felt the same way he did, and finding out that he was just your release from tension probably crushed him."

Ayanna couldn't answer. Billie hit the nail squarely on the head, and hearing it like that made Ayanna feel small and dirty. Billie's private line started ringing and she rose to take the call. Ayanna escaped the office like the sniveling coward she'd turned out to be. Just when she'd thought she couldn't feel any worse, she'd found out how wrong she was.

Chapter 14

The next three weeks were sheer hell. She and Billie eventually made up, but the first few days of working together were rough. Billie had apparently filled Dakota and Toni in on the breakup because they discreetly didn't mention it. Not that Ayanna saw them much; she made excuses to miss any suggested outings with her friends, and they always seemed to work, for which she was grateful. The hard part was to turn off the waterworks because for some reason crying relieved the pain, even though it was only a temporary respite. She forced herself to stay dry-eyed and stoic. It was sometimes impossible, especially when she was around Billie, and since they saw each other five days a week, it was doubly tough. They were over their tense discussion, but Ayanna still felt uneasy. She was sad that her friend was having morning sickness, but it did serve as a distraction, like today.

Billie came out of the office bathroom looking pale. She was wiping her face with paper towels and moaning. "If I read one more interview with some damned actress talking about how she never had morning sickness even though she was carrying sextuplets, I'ma go to Hollywood and beat the bitch *down*," she said savagely. "Being pregnant is hard. Nobody tells you how miserable it is. They just tell you how wonderful it is to have a beautiful baby," she sniffed.

Ayanna sympathized. "Did Dakota have morning sickness?"

Billie brightened. "Yes, she did. She felt like hell for three months. She's a good sister," Billie said as she reached for the saltines that were never far away.

"Let me get you some ginger ale," Ayanna said solicitously.

"Lots of ice, please, and a little water." Even the soothing ginger ale could cause a riot in tummy town for Billie, so she usually watered it down a little.

Ayanna came back from the break room with the ice-filled glass and a paper-wrapped straw. "Here you go, Billie."

Billie brightened and took the glass. "You're a lifesaver," she sighed. "So when are you going to pick up the boys?"

"Next week. School doesn't start for three weeks, but Cameron has preseason practice with the football team. And we have school shopping to do." She shuddered. Back-to-school shopping was expensive and tedious. She thought about the crowds of harried mothers all searching for the best items at the best prices, hordes of pouting children who wanted something way outside the family budget that would also flout the school dress code. Not to mention the long lines of shoppers at the cash register. She wished with all her heart she could have done it earlier, but with growing boys, there was no point in trying to buy their clothes ahead of time.

"It's too bad Johnny won't be here to help you drive," Billie said.

Ayanna was jerked out of her negative thoughts by Billie's words.

"What do you mean?"

"Oh, you didn't know, I guess. Sorry. Anyway, Johnny's going to Africa next week, and then he has to go to Switzerland and England after that. This is the longest trip he's made in a while. We won't see him until Halloween, probably, if then. I think he has something going on in New York when he gets back from the U.K." She belched loudly and begged Ayanna's pardon. "I'm so sorry, honey. I'm not trying to be rude, but this baby must be a soccer player. It just kicks the gas out of me. I'm going to my office to rattle the walls in private."

Ayanna was glad of the privacy because she wasn't sure she could hold back the tears. He was going away without a word to her. After the way she'd behaved, she couldn't blame him. She'd made such a mess of things, and she had no idea how to get things back together. The only good thing was that she wasn't pregnant. Her period had finally come. Just as she'd hoped, it was a cycle change that caused her to be so late. It had taken her three days to finally e-mail him, as he requested. He didn't even bother to answer, which was to be expected.

The really sad thing was that she was still madly in love with him. She still believed she wasn't the right woman for him, no matter what he said in a moment of passion. She just couldn't settle for an affair, and he couldn't commit to marriage. She'd heard him say so too many times, and she'd heard it from his sisters, too. Even when Billie was dressing her down about the way things had ended, she never said that Johnny wanted to marry her. So she'd had a little taste of love and she'd savor it for the rest of her life because she knew she'd never feel anything like it again.

Anyone who knew him well would know that Johnny was in a foul mood. His sisters, praise Jesus, were busy with their own lives, and he'd managed to duck and dodge them for the last couple of weeks. Dakota was busy with the baby, and Billie was deep in the throes of constant morning sickness so he was able to successfully claim that he was busy at work, which was true. He welcomed the travel that lay ahead of him because he wanted out of Chicago with a vengeance.

Why the hell had he taken a job that would put him in the same city as that deceitful little wench?

He was in a place he despised—O'Hare Airport— while he mulled this over. True, he hadn't known that he was going to get involved with Ayanna. And he hadn't known that all his faculties would desert him once he did. The bitterness boiled up in him again as he thought about how she'd fooled him completely. The first time he really fell in love and all she wanted was a good time. The irony made him smile grimly, an expression that frightened the hell out of two little old ladies who were approaching the area where he was sitting. They turned around and went the other way, but he didn't notice them.

His flight was finally called, and he went to the gate with all his boarding papers in one hand and his new laptop over his shoulder in its leather carrying case. He'd had to purchase it when the other one broke. "Broke" wasn't the right description; when he'd gotten the one-line e-mail from Ayanna that read "not pregnant," he'd smashed the expensive computer into pieces.

He stowed his carry-on under his seat and hung his sport coat in the first class locker area before sitting down. He always paid the difference between business class and first class because of his long legs. He had a lot of flying to do, and he wasn't in the mood for a stiff back and cramped legs. He had fastened his seat belt and closed his eyes to await take off, when he could recline his seat and go to sleep. He was hoping he could get some sleep on the plane because he wasn't doing much of it in Nick's garish apartment. He despised that horrible bed and everything it represented, since it made him think of Ayanna. She was the last person he wanted to think about in this life.

A sultry voice roused him. "I think this is my seat. Would you prefer the aisle? We can switch if you like."

He opened his eyes to see a statuesque woman with a thick head of long hair standing next to the aisle seat. "Sure. That's very thoughtful of you," he said as he undid his seat belt and stood up.

They switched places, and he felt the warmth from her curvy body and smelled her perfume. He gave her a quick glance before sitting down. If this was his companion all the way to London where he would change planes, life had just gotten a lot more pleasant.

"I'm Celeste Brown," she said, offering him a hand.

"John Phillips." Her hand was soft and warm, and she looked like an intelligent, charming seatmate. Yes, things were looking better already.

Chapter 15

Ayanna had always enjoyed driving long distances, but not this trip. She drove steadily, listening to NPR all the way down to South Carolina because music of all kinds just served to remind her of Johnny and the love she still had for him. Even though it meant she would probably never see him again, she was happy he was out of the country because it would make it easier to transition the boys out of the relationship. With him out of the country for a few months, they would gradually get used to his absence and the fact that he was no longer a part of their lives.

She was hoping that the excitement of school, with football practice for Cameron and band practice for Alec, would keep them from noticing how bad she looked. She was losing weight, and it showed. She looked anorexic, and to an extent she was, because she just couldn't bear eating. She made herself eat because she had to, but it was as pleasurable as eating gravel. She just hoped her mother wouldn't notice how haggard she was. Nothing much got past Lucie Porter.

The drive wasn't horrible, although the gas prices were astronomical. She had already set money aside for the trip, and it was a good thing that she always budgeted on the high side or she might have been stranded on the side of the road. She made the trip in thirteen hours, stopping only to fill up the tank and her thermos cup with coffee. Her mouth was puckered and bitter from all the brew she'd consumed, but it would all be over soon. She'd already passed the sign that indicated the exit for Columbia was coming up. She popped a few Altoids in her mouth and tried to school her face into a pleasant expression, a lighthearted look of carefree happiness. When she pulled into her mother's driveway she could feel what a failure the effort was. Her sunken cheeks actually hurt from the effort of trying to smile, but she did her best.

"Hi, Ma!" Cameron and Alec leaped off the porch and grabbed her.

"Let me look at you," she exclaimed. "Good heavens, I think you grew three inches, Alec!"

"Two and a half, Ma," he said proudly. "Cameron only grew two inches."

"Yeah, but my feet got a size bigger," Cameron boasted.

With her arms around her boys' waists, she went up the stairs to greet her mother. "Hi, Mommy!" she said in a too-cheery voice.

Lucie just raised an eyebrow. "We'll talk later. Boys, get your mother's things out of the car, please."

She hugged Ayanna tightly, making a face when she felt how thin she was. "I made you your favorite rhubarb pie," she said comfortingly. "You're a little thin, aren't you, dear?"

The tears started running before Ayanna could stop them.

"Go on upstairs. I'll get the boys to set the table or something," Lucie said.

Ayanna gladly went upstairs to her mother's bedroom. She threw herself across the bed and waited for Lucie to come talk to her. The faint scent of Giorgio was in the room, as always. In a couple of minutes, Lucie was in the doorway with a bowl of rhubarb pie topped with ice cream in one hand and a glass of iced tea in the other hand.

"Life is short, honey. Eat dessert first," she quipped.

Ayanna sat up and crossed her legs like she'd done when she was little, and her mother handed her the bowl of pie.

"Tell me what happened, Ayanna. I could tell something was bothering you from your phone calls, but I was going to wait until I saw you to dig it out of you. Now I can see with my own eyes that something's wrong, and if I'm not mistaken, it has something to do with that magnificent specimen, doesn't it?"

"Yes, it does." Ayanna swallowed hard to get rid of the lump in her throat. She told Lucie all about her fight with Johnny and how he'd reacted. Lucie listened closely, and when Ayanna wound down, she reached out to take Ayanna's hand.

"Sweetie pie, you know I love you to pieces, but I'm afraid this is more about you than it is about him." She held a hand up to stop the indignant response Ayanna was about to deliver. "Ayanna, you're my daughter, and I know you better than anyone, so I have to ask, what in the world made you think you weren't good enough for that man? You got stuck on stupid, honey. You planted this seed of doubt in your head, and you let it flourish into a big plant instead of plucking that lie out of your head and tossing it aside.

"Who on earth told you that the only women he gets involved with are the doctors and lawyers and Indian chiefs? Sounds to me like they're the ones he goes though like a box of tissues. How did you get to have such a poor self-image that you think you can't be the answer to somebody's prayer?" Lucie was really wound up now, and she started walking around the room, the way she always did when she was excited.

"I'm going to tell you something I thought you already knew. Men don't know who they're going to marry until the woman lets them know. They can't make up their minds about what they want for break-fast much less who they're going to spend the rest of their lives with. Now this man has spent his whole life running from fast women, and when he meets you, he knows you're the one because that's the message you sent out there to the universe. He just knew in his heart that you were the right one." She stopped pacing long enough to stroke Ayanna's face and then pat her head.

"When a man like Johnny loves, he loves hard. He puts everything into making you happy. Couldn't you tell how he felt about you? I could, but that's not the issue." She started winding down at last and sat down on the bed again.

"Well, you're just going to have to get him back," Lucie said firmly. She held up her hand again to cut Ayanna off. "I don't know how you're going to do it. You're a smart woman. You'll figure it out. But you're just going to have to get him back. That's my son-in-law," she said. "I want him in my family."

Ayanna almost choked on the sweet sassafras tea. "But, Mommy, he's gone to Africa. He might not come back, ever."

Lucie stood up grandly and gave Ayanna the look that said "don't be ridiculous." "Honey, everything and everyone comes back. Besides, Africa is just a plane ride away. When you finish your pie, come on down for dinner. I made smothered chicken and succotash with angel biscuits."

As improbable as it seemed, after fifteen minutes in her mother's house, Ayanna felt better. What her mother said made a lot of sense, as usual. She had been stuck on stupid. She had planted the seed of unworthiness in her head and let the resulting poisoned vine choke off all her common sense. Nobody could have treated her like Johnny had unless he loved her the same way she loved him. And he had to know she loved him.... Or maybe not. She had been screaming at him like an idiot the last time she'd seen him.

She polished off the last of the delicious tart pie and gulped the iced tea. Suddenly she realized she was still hungry. Smothered chicken and angel biscuits sounded like the perfect thing to her. She was going to get her appetite back. And maybe, if her mother had anything to say about it, she would get her man back, too.

She pattered down the stairs and went into the kitchen. "Everything smells so good! Do you need help with anything?"

Lucie smiled and patted her cheek. "Not a thing, Ayanna. Just sit down and eat. Eat a *lot*."

Johnny looked at his seatmate for the tenth time. She had been pleasant but quiet, and she'd been typing steadily on a thing that was the size of a laptop but it looked like a weird typewriter of sorts. He finally had to ask what it was.

"This? It's my AlphaSmart," she said and laughed. "All I can do is type on it so I stay focused on my manuscript. I can't be trusted with my laptop because I'll start reading e-mail or checking out things on the Internet, and before I realize it, I'm staring down my deadline like a deer caught in the headlights. This way all I can do is write."

"So you're a writer. What do you write?"

She gave him a sexy, playful smile. "I write

romance. I also write murder mysteries. I'll bet you don't read much romance."

"Actually, I've read a few. I thought I knew your name from somewhere. My lady loves romance novels, and you're one of her favorite authors." He paused and his expression changed. "My former lady, I should say."

"You just broke up, didn't you?"

Johnny gave her a half smile that couldn't have fooled anyone. "Are you psychic, or does it show?"

"Well, my husband thinks I'm psychic because he says I can read his mind, but really the look is all too familiar. That's how I looked before I got married. We had a terrible falling out, and we called off the wedding."

Johnny grimaced again. "Well, I don't have to worry about that because I never got around to proposing. This was a clean break."

Celeste gave him a good once over. "I don't think so. I think this really hurt you, and if she has half the feelings you have, she's probably just as miserable."

"I doubt that. She was interested in one thing only— sex. She wasn't into having a relationship or anything close to it. She'd been cooling her heels for eleven years, and I was her summer stud. She sent her boys off to her mom's for vacation, and then she and I got busy. When I called her on it, it blew up in her face, and it was over."

Celeste looked concerned and caring. "This is going to be a long flight. Why don't you start at the beginning, and tell me all about it. I think you might be missing a few elements in your assessment of the situation," she said.

"There's really nothing to tell," Johnny said, and for the next four hours, he told her the long version of "nothing."

Celeste waved to the attendant who was serving first class. "I'm getting a glass of wine, and I think you should, too," she said to Johnny. "You could really use one."

Johnny gave a rough laugh that didn't sound amused. "This must be your worst nightmare," he said. "To be trapped on a crazy-long flight with a lovesick fool."

Celeste patted his hand. "Let me tell you something. There's nothing wrong with being lovesick. It's better than being heartless. And whether you realize it or not, your lady's heart is broken, too. I don't know how you leapt to the conclusion that she was just using that big fine body of yours for sex, but I can tell you with all the authority vested in me by the Romance Writers of America that it's just not so. Your Ayanna loves you with all her heart." She smiled as their server brought her a chilled glass of chardonnay and insisted that he take a sip of his merlot.

"You need to mellow out a little. Now then, let's go over what you just told me. Remember, I love mysteries and romance, and this is a little of both," she told him. "First of all, she's a good woman. She gave up her career dreams to raise her sister's kids without complaint. She lost a fiancé in the process, although personally, I think she didn't lose much.

"She works hard, her life revolves around her kids, she's helpful and kind and she was celibate. In no court of law would she be found to be anything but a good woman, John. And from the pictures you showed me on your BlackBerry, she's lovely. She could have had plenty of sex if she wanted to. Why do you think she waited for you?"

Johnny thought about it and before he could come up with an answer, Celeste was talking again. "This lady loves romance. She loves to dance. She loves to cook for people she loves. She put her dreams on hold and her life, too. She could have had a very different life, but it wasn't in the cards, so she did the best with what she could. And then comes you."

Their server brought their meal, and as they began to eat the surprisingly well-cooked prime rib, Celeste continued to educate him. "John, I'm not ashamed to tell you that if I wasn't about to celebrate my silver anniversary with the man I've adored since I was nineteen, you'd tempt even me. So poor Ayanna had to have been swept off her feet.

"But she's so humble and down-to-earth it never occurred to her that an international lover like you would be interested in settling down with a homebody like her. She was taking what she could get, John, because she thought that's all there was."

"But she should have known how I felt, Celeste. I never held anything back from her."

"Did you tell her you loved her? Aside from the night you were fighting, that is."

"Well, no," Johnny admitted.

"Did you discuss the future, marriage, what your role as stepfather to her sons would be? Where you would live, what her role would be as your wife, what your hopes and expectations were about a life with her?"

"Well, no, I didn't," he said slowly.

"So exactly how was she supposed to know how you felt? You're talking about a woman with relatively little experience in dating. The experience she had was ten years out of date, and you expected her to be some kind of love psychic because you had good sex? Does that make sense to you?"

The things Celeste was saying in her friendly, down-to-earth way were so simple that he felt like a jackass for not thinking of them himself.

He asked the flight attendant for another glass of wine. He had a feeling he might have yet another before the flight was over.

"And remember, John. This all blew up because you gave her an impulsive gift that she thought was too expensive. A skank would've taken the bling and run with it, but she really cared about you spending money frivolously. She loved you too much for that."

"Celeste, you really are special. I can see why you've had a romance that's lasted so long. Your husband is a lucky man."

"We're a lucky couple. But don't get it twisted.

We've had our share of ups and downs over the years. I told you we'd broken off the engagement at one point."

"Yeah, but you didn't say what happened. Tell me about it." Johnny invited.

And for the next couple of hours, she did.

Chapter 16

Ayanna was so happy to see her boys that it took the edge off her misery. She'd missed Alec and Cameron terribly, and they'd missed her, although they'd had a wonderful summer. Lucie, bless her heart, had a surprise for her. She was deeply grateful to her mother for doing their school shopping before she came to get them. The time it was going to save her was worth gold, in her estimation. Plus, her mother refused to accept payment for the clothes and shoes. She had fussed at Ayanna in her loving way.

"Ayanna, don't be ridiculous! You never did know how to take things from anyone. You're so independent it borders on fanaticism. When your father died, he didn't leave me destitute. I've always worked and had my own money, my own savings. And he left us money as well. Since you were smart enough to get full scholarships, your college money has just been gaining interest. It was supposed to support you while you were in Paris at the Cordon Bleu, but you didn't go, and the money's just sitting around," Lucie said.

They were on the back porch sipping coffee after breakfast the day after Ayanna arrived. "Why didn't you tell me this before?" she asked her mother.

"I did tell you, but I think you were too distraught to take it in. I just held on to it because it would be there for you when you needed it for something. I figured the insurance money from Attiya was tiding you over."

Attiya was her sister, Alec and Cameron's birth mother. "Mommy, I put that money in trust for Alec and Cameron. I've never touched it. It's just sitting there gaining interest," she said. "And before you say anything, I did tell you I was going to do that. I told Daddy, and that was just like telling you."

They looked at each other and laughed. Lucie had to get in the last word, though. "The point is you deserve to have a little relief in your life. You have worked like a Hebrew slave to take care of my grandsons, and I couldn't be more proud of the job you've done. But at some point you've got to take some time for yourself. Buy an outfit that isn't on clearance and some shoes that aren't from Payless. Let your hair grow out. I know you keep it short so you can do it yourself to save money, but you deserve to pamper yourself a little. I'm going to give you some of that inheritance so that you can have a little more wiggle room in your budget." Lucie stood and poured her now cold coffee on the flowers that surrounded the porch. "Besides, you might need to go to Africa one of these days."

Ayanna shook her head as she followed her mother into the house to begin packing the boys for the trip home. She could appreciate her mother's optimism; she just needed a dose of her vision. Right now, she just couldn't see how a reunion with Johnny was going to happen.

It was wonderful having her boys back home. She was so busy she didn't have time to mope. She was back to the usual routine of taking them to school, packing lunches, attending parent-teacher conferences and the like that her days were too full to think about Johnny. The nights were a different situation, because he haunted her dreams in ways that she desired to be rid of, but there was nothing she could do about that.

She was leaving work early today for Cameron's first official game of the season. Preseason was over, and there'd been a couple of nonconference games, but this was the first one that would count. She'd been a little concerned about him lately because he seemed to be somewhat listless and tired, but he assured her he was fine.

"I have some tough classes this semester, and between studying and football practice, I've just been kinda tired. I'll start taking vitamins. That should do it."

She looked into his eyes and felt his forehead that

very morning. "You seem a little warm to me," she said. "I'm making an appointment for you with Dr. Brady."

"Aw, Ma," he said, scratching the back of his neck.

"Why do you have that bandage on? Did you hurt your arm?"

"This? No, it's just a spider bite. It's been itching a lot, though, so I put some Neosporin on it and covered it up so it wouldn't get dirty."

"Let me see." she reached for his arm but he pulled away.

"Ma, look at it when I get home. C'mon, we're gonna be late, and I need to talk to my chemistry teacher before class."

She let him get away with it and promised herself that she'd look at it carefully that evening. After a busy day of work, she picked up Alec from school, and they had the rare treat of burgers and fries at their favorite greasy spoon before the game. She was really touched to see Nick and Jason in the stands. "I'm so glad to see you," she said. "How are Bethany and Dakota?"

"They're fine," Nick said. "Dakota was just saying that it's been too long since she's seen you. She wants you to come for dinner soon."

She promised that she would, and she and Alec sat down to cheer Cameron on. The game went well; their team won and Cameron made a touchdown, which thrilled Alec to no end. After the game, though, Cameron still seemed listless and didn't want to go to a party, nor did he want something to eat.

"I'm just gonna crash, Ma. See you in the morning."

It was too late to check his arm, but Ayanna vowed she was going to corral him first thing in the morning.

This time she didn't forget. She practically pounced on him before he got out of bed, and she took off the bandage. She tried not to let her panic show, but she didn't like the looks of it at all. His arm was swollen and red, and there was a nasty ooze of pus that looked terribly infected. *Spider bite, my foot. This looks like a tarantula chomped him.*

Suddenly she didn't want to wait for her appointment with the doctor; she wanted him seen that day. "Why don't you get up and take a shower, sweetie? I'm going to have that arm looked at today. No arguments, Cameron. Shower now, please."

She went right to the phone and called Todd Wainwright. Besides being Billie's brother-in-law and head of the emergency room at John Stroger Hospital, he was a good friend of Ayanna's. He would tell her what to do for Cameron.

She was pleased when she got him on the phone right away, and she explained his symptoms. God bless him, he was a comfort to her right away. "It's probably nothing, but go ahead and bring him in, Ayanna. I'll meet you in the emergency room. Just ask for me at the desk, and I'll let them know you're coming in."

Ayanna made sure that Alec bathed and dressed, too. "I'd rather you come with me than stay here by yourself. It's not going to take long, and we can go get something to eat afterward," she said.

"Sounds good to me, Ma." Alec was always ready to eat.

When they got to the emergency room, it wasn't too crowded. Ayanna went to the admitting desk and said her name, adding that Dr. Todd Wainwright was expecting her. The person at the desk told her to have a seat and someone would be with her shortly. Sure enough, Todd came to get her in a few minutes. He was tall, dark and handsome and the object of many a woman's desire, but he was too busy working to settle down in a relationship. He was dedicated to his profession.

"Hello, Ayanna, Cameron, Alec. Cameron, I understand you're not feeling too well. Come with me, and let me take a look."

He took Cameron into an examining room and Ayanna followed. Cameron sat on the edge of the uncomfortable cot and rolled up his sleeve when Todd asked him to. Todd held his arm and examined it closely, then he put his arm down and looked in his eyes, his ears and down his throat, asking him questions the whole time. "Are you tired more than usual? How's your appetite? Playing sports this year? Oh yeah, which one? Good for you, that's great. Lie down, and let me listen to your heart," he said. He listened in several places and had Cameron take deep breaths, cough and pant rapidly.

"Cameron, somebody's going to come in and take some blood from you in a few minutes. Your mom and I will be right back, okay?"

Todd took her elbow and led her out into the hallway. "Ayanna, I'm going to cut to the chase. Cameron has MRSA."

Ayanna thought she might faint. She could literally feel the blood draining from her face. "That super-bug staph infection? Are you sure, Todd?" She'd read several tragic stories about children Cameron's age who'd died from the disease. It had been referred to as a pandemic in the media, and all the news she'd heard about it was bad.

"I'm as sure as I can be without the lab work. We'll know for sure shortly. But the spider bite on his arm is definitely a staph infection. The infection mimics other things like a boil or pimple or insect bite, and it often doesn't get diagnosed until it's had a chance to really infect the patient."

"But how could he get this thing?" Ayanna was trying hard to hold it together, but she was terrified by what she was hearing.

"Staph infections are fairly common. Even MRSA is fairly common, but it used to be confined to hospitals, nursing homes, places where people are exposed to bacteria and viruses on a daily basis. This new strain can be found in schools, Ayanna, especially in locker rooms. We don't know why, but the bacteria flourish there. A person could get a little scratch during football practice, and then the person could touch someone who may be a host or some piece of equipment that the host has handled and the person could get the infection. The problem is that this strain is resistant to antibiotics."

Ayanna looked like she was about to pass out, and Todd put his arm around her shoulder to support her. "I'm going to admit Cameron to the hospital because he definitely has pneumonia, which is an escalating symptom of MRSA. What we want to do is start treatment as quickly as possible to increase the odds that he'll be back playing ball in a week or two. Okay?"

Ayanna nodded her head. "Just get him well, Todd. Just get him well."

"And you know this," Todd said. "He's young and healthy, and he's going to fight this thing. What I need you to do now is go to Admissions and get the paperwork going. When you're done, I'll come and get you and bring you to Cameron."

"Okay. I need to get Alec, I don't want him to be in the waiting room by himself," she murmured.

"Is there anyone I can call for you, Ayanna? I don't want you to be here alone, either."

"Oh no, there's no one here but me and the boys. I mean, my family is in South Carolina. I'm fine, really. Where is the admitting office?"

She went to collect Alec, and they made the trip to the office. She was trying to hold it together for the sake of her sons, but it was hard. She caught a glimpse of Alec's face and forced herself to smile. "This won't take too long, and then we can go see Cameron," she said.

"Is he really sick? I mean really, really sick, Ma?" He sounded so young and frightened that Ayanna found the strength to reassure him.

"He has an infection, and Todd is going to do his

best to get it cleared up. He's in good hands, Alec. He's going to be fine." As they approached the office, she prayed with all her heart that her words were true.

Chapter 17

Despite Todd's optimistic and comforting words, Cameron's lab results not only confirmed the diagnosis of MRSA, but it showed that the disease was affecting his internal organs. Within twenty-four hours, he was moved into intensive care, and Ayanna had a glimpse of what hell must be like. Todd had wisely informed Billie and Jason that Cameron had been hospitalized, and Jason showed up at the hospital with Nick shortly after his initial admission.

They hugged Ayanna, who was trying to stay as calm as possible. "Look, I'm not going to tell you what Billie said, but the gist of it was that she's a little peeved that you didn't let her know. She's still battling the morning sickness or she'd be here herself," Jason told her.

"Dakota didn't want to bring Bethany out in the rain, or she'd be here, too," Nick said. His green eyes were warm with concern. "She says we're family, and she doesn't appreciate you treating us like strangers." He hugged her again as her eyes filled with tears. "Look, I'm going to take Alec with me. He doesn't need to be here for all this. We'll get him fed and get clothes from your house and all that. You look like you could use some food, too."

Ayanna shook her head and said she was fine. "To be honest, I don't think I could keep anything down. But thank you for asking," she murmured. "Alec, why don't you get your jacket and go with Nick. I know you must be starving, and you look like you could use some rest."

"But what about you, Ma? You need some rest, too," he protested.

"Sweetie, I'm fine. I'm a superwoman. Don't worry about me. I need to stay here with Cameron to make sure he's all right. I'll call you as soon as I know something."

She hugged him tightly and found it difficult to let go. With an effort that was truly superhuman, she smiled at him and said she'd see him soon. She watched him walk away with Nick and started trembling. Jason put his arm around her waist and hugged her to his side. "Hang in there, kid. Come on and sit down. I'm going to go get you something to eat, and you're going to eat it, too."

Jason stayed with her until she insisted that he go

home and see about Billie. "Tell her I'm sorry I didn't call. It's just that things were happening so fast, I didn't think about it."

"Have you called your mother? She's not going to be any happier than Billie or Dakota if she finds out about this later," he pointed out.

"You're right, I should call her. But I have to go downstairs to use my cell phone, and I just don't want to leave him in case the doctors have something to tell me or he gets worse…" Her voice trailed off.

"You go downstairs and make the call. I'll stay right here, and if we need you, I'll call you," Jason said firmly.

"Okay, I will. Thanks, Jason. Thank you so much."

She went down to the lobby and out the front doors. She needed some fresh air desperately. It was raining, like Nick had said. She had lost all track of the time or the day. She tried to think and realized it had been over twenty-four hours since she'd brought Cameron to the hospital. She was holding her cell phone so tightly it hurt her hand. She moved it from one hand to the other and flexed her cramped fingers. She pushed a few buttons and was soon listening to her mother's voice.

"Mommy, I've got some bad news. Cameron is in the hospital. He has MRSA, and it has invaded his, um, his internal organs."

She didn't start crying until Lucie said, "I'll be there on the next plane. Hang on, honey, I'm coming."

When Ayanna went back to the waiting area, she was stunned to find Cameron's football coach, his school principal and his closest friends in the waiting area talking to Jason. The coach's name was Nathan Bridges and he was a tall, handsome fellow whose concern was plain to see.

"Ms. Porter, I heard that Cameron was sick, and I wanted to let you know how sorry we were to hear about it. He's a great young man, and if there's anything I can do to help, I'll be more than happy to do it. His teammates are really concerned about him, in fact the whole school is," he told her.

The principal, Mrs. Carter, agreed. "Cameron is such a lovely young man. He has a brilliant future ahead of him, and we're praying that he gets well soon."

His friends, Zack and Anthony, weren't as polished as the adults, but they hugged Ayanna and asked if they could do anything to help.

"Just pray for him. If you all would just keep praying," she said, "I think God will hear all our prayers and answer them."

To her surprise, the coach took her hand and held out his other one, and Anthony took it without hesitation. They formed a circle with Jason, and he said a simple but well-worded prayer that was so comforting to Ayanna that for the first time she didn't feel like crying. She felt something that she really needed, which was hope.

Lucie looked around the waiting area, which was full of flowers and teddy bears and school mascots and get-well cards, and pressed her hand to her cheek. One of the chairs was completely taken over with the bounty of tributes that Cameron's teachers, classmates and teammates had brought, and it was clear that Ayanna had been in the same position for the seventy-two hours that had passed since Cameron's admittance to the intensive care unit.

"Ayanna, honey, you've got to go home," Lucie pleaded. "You need a hot bath and some real sleep. You can't keep hovering around here napping in these waiting room chairs. And you've got to get the flowers and things out of here. It's too hard for the nurses to deal with all this. It needs to be at your house. That's why I'm here, sweetie pie, to handle things so you can get some rest. Go home for just a few hours, and come back later. You're not alone anymore. Mommy is here, honey."

Ayanna knew what her mother was saying made sense, but she couldn't bring herself to do as she suggested. She was so riddled with guilt and anxiety that she couldn't think straight. When her mother had come into the waiting area she'd finally broken down in her arms. After a brief cry, she resumed her stoic posture, but Lucie had seen right through it. It was time for tough love.

Billie, Dakota, Toni and their husbands had all come up to sit with Ayanna, fetch her food and just support her. She was never alone now, but she couldn't bring herself to leave. Lucie had to turn into a drill sergeant to get her out of there.

"Ayanna Demetria Porter, you are going to listen to me and do what I say. Billie is going to take you home, and you are going to take a hot shower. Dakota has made you a meal, and you are going to sit down and eat it. And then you are going to sleep in your own bed," she said in her sternest department-head voice.

"But, Mommy," she began.

Lucie almost stamped her foot in frustration. "Baby girl, take that word out of your vocabulary. There is no 'but' around here except the one you sit on. Alec is worried half to death because he hasn't seen you, and you have to remember that if you fall, the whole family falls. You must keep up your strength."

Lucie took her by the hand and led her over to Billie. "Please take her home, Billie. Sit on her if you have to, but keep her there, please. And can Jason or somebody please put all this stuff in your car and take it to the house later?"

Billie set her jaw and assured Lucie that she would do whatever it took to get Ayanna to cooperate. "She'll do it or else. Come on, sister girl. Enough with the dumb stuff, I'm taking you home right now. Jason will get all the flowers and things."

Ayanna just nodded her head numbly and went along.

She didn't think it was possible, but she really did feel better after a few hours. The shower felt wonderful. She scrubbed herself over and over with her bath puff and copious amounts of bath gel. Afterward, she applied lotion and body butter because her skin felt so dry and neglected. She didn't have enough energy to get dressed, but it didn't matter because Dakota brought her a tray.

"Here you go, Ayanna. I know it's the middle of the afternoon, but if you're like me you can eat breakfast any time of the day or night. It's just so comforting."

"You're so right, Dakota. This looks delicious," she said with a smile. It wasn't her usual big dimpled smile, but it was a start.

Dakota had made her scrambled eggs with toast, creamy grits, bacon and sausage and fried apples. There was a big glass of orange juice and a cup of tea. Ayanna suddenly realized she was starving and started eating everything on the tray.

"This is so good," she said. "I can't thank you enough."

"You don't have to thank me, girl! It was my pleasure. I would have made you some biscuits, but that is not one of my skills," she added dryly. They talked until Ayanna had finished every bite. Dakota took the tray and told her to sleep for a while.

"You really need this rest. Your mom is there, and Cameron is getting the best possible treatment. Sleep while you can."

And to her surprise, Ayanna was able to drift off for a much-needed nap. When she woke up, Alec was sitting in the chair looking lost. There was a book in his lap, but he hadn't been reading it.

"Hey, sweetie. Come give me a kiss," she said.

She sat up, and he came over to give her a big hug and a kiss on the cheek.

"How are you feeling, Ma?"

"I'm better now that I see you." She smiled and gave him another squeeze. For once he didn't back away and protest the mushy stuff; he let her hold him.

"Ma, is Cameron going to die?" His voice broke as he asked the question.

"No, he's not," she said fiercely. "He's not going to die. We're going to pray about it right now, okay?"

They held hands tightly and prayed for God's healing protection for Cameron.

Lucie didn't really want her to go back to the hospital, but Ayanna couldn't stay away. She'd showered, changed clothes, eaten and rested and she was back. They let her put on a paper gown, gloves and mask to go into intensive care to see him, but she could only go in for fifteen minutes at a time. It didn't matter, though. Fifteen minutes was better than nothing. Cameron looked so young and helpless as he slept. He was basically unconscious most of the time. The medication wasn't working yet, and Todd had told her that he might have to undergo surgery to clear the infection from his internal organs, especially his lungs.

She was frightened beyond reason, but she controlled her fear. Todd introduced her to the surgeon who would be operating on Cameron, if necessary, and to the infectious disease specialist. Everyone was very kind and professional, but it didn't ease her mind as much as her continual prayers. Lucie had reminded her that He was still in the miracle business and that it was only His word that mattered.

Ayanna was alone now. She didn't really mind because she needed to be near Cameron, and she needed the solitude to pray. The lights in the waiting area were dimmed because it was so late. She wasn't sure but she thought it was midnight or close to it. She wasn't completely sure what day it was. Lucie was at home with Alec, and Billie and Dakota were at home with their husbands. It was quiet and almost peaceful, even though she was trying to curl up in a decidedly hard chair.

She was cold and uncomfortable and wished she had a pillow or something. She could ask the nurses, but she didn't want to bother them. They had enough to do. She wrapped her arms around herself and rocked back and forth. She was thinking about the possibility that her baby would have to undergo major surgery, and she clasped her hands and put them to her mouth. Her thoughts became overwhelming, and she stood up and started to pace. She thought she heard someone say her name, but she figured she was hearing things.

She heard it again and turned around to see Johnny walking toward her. She stood still, not believing her eyes until he reached her and put his arms around her, holding her tight.

"Baby, I'm so sorry. I'm so sorry," he whispered.

She didn't hear his words. She was too caught up in the fact that he was there and he was holding her. She looked at him with dazed eyes. "I'm not dreaming, am I? You're really here, aren't you?" she said shakily.

"I'm right here, sweetness. I'll always be here for you."

Ayanna buried her head in his comforting shoulder and held on for dear life.

Chapter 18

"How did you know?" Ayanna asked when she was finally able to stop holding him. He walked her over to the unyielding sofa and sat down, keeping one arm around her and holding her hand. "Billie called me. Then Dakota called me. My mother called me. Jason called me. I was already on my way to the airport by the time my mother got on the phone," he said.

"I can't believe you're really here," she said softly. "I'm so scared, Johnny."

"I know you are, sweetheart, but this isn't in our hands anymore. It's all up to God, and He's going to take care of our boy." She nodded and looked at him with absolute trust in her eyes. He kissed her on each cheek and on her lips, very gently. "Tell me what happened, Ayanna."

She told him about Cameron's listlessness and his lack of appetite and about the day she'd noticed the bandage. "When he was little he'd run to me with every scratch," she said sadly. "I was too busy and too caught up in my own misery to even notice that my child had a staph infection," she said brokenly. "By the time I actually saw it, I knew something was wrong, and I brought him to the E.R. so Todd could take a look, and he's been here ever since. The infection has spread to his internal organs, and they're probably going to operate on him tomorrow because he's not responding to any of the medications. MRSA is resistant to antibiotics," she said, and then she looked embarrassed. "Why am I telling you this? You probably know more about it than some of the doctors around here."

He stroked the side of her face and kissed her again. He did know more than the average person about a lot of infectious diseases because of the nature of his work, but he'd hardly consider himself to be an expert.

"Will they let me see him?"

"Yes, but not yet. Visiting hours don't start until nine, and you can only go in fifteen minutes at a time. You'll have to say you're family, though. Only family members can visit."

"I am family," he said. "You're my family, you and Alec and Cameron. You're the woman I love, Ayanna. I know we made a mess of things, but that's the past and from here on out, we're only concerned with the future. No more misunderstandings, no more screwups. I love you."

"I love you, too. I love you so much, and I thought—
Never mind what I thought. I love you, Johnny. It was
never just sex for me."

"I know that, baby." He stole another kiss and then
gave her the devilish grin. "But the sex was good, wasn't
it?"

"You are a sick, sick man."

"That may be true, but I'm *your* man, and don't you
ever forget it."

Nick arrived to spell Ayanna for a while so she could
stretch her legs and get some coffee. While he knew she
probably wouldn't do either, he wanted to check on her.
When he came around the corner and saw her holding
hands with Johnny, he frowned.

"It's about time you got here. Your mama and daddy
are here. I just picked them up at the airport, and since
I was already up, I came on over here to see about my
girl. You better call your folks because they're about to
disown you," he said dryly.

"Good to see you, too, bro. Aren't you glad you
married my sister? See what a fun family we are?"
Johnny shook his brother-in-law's hand and smiled.

Nick grinned back. "You got the best family in the
world, and I'm a part of it so show some love. Take this
poor woman out of here for a while, and I'll hold it
down here."

"I have something for you."

Ayanna was across from Johnny in a big booth at an
all-night diner near the hospital. Her face turned red and

she looked panicked. Johnny reached into the pocket of his sport coat and pulled out a paperback book. "Don't get scared, it's just a book."

He slid it across the table, and she picked it up with curious hands. "This is a Celeste Brown book. It's not due out for two months. How did you get it?"

"I met her on a flight to London on my way to Africa. She sat next to me on the plane, and we talked about you for seven hours."

"You didn't!" Ayanna was really blushing now. Her face looked as hot as fire.

"Yes, we did, sweetness. I told her all about you and how I messed everything up between us. I owe you a big apology, Ayanna. I want you to know how sorry I am that I hurt you. It's the last thing I ever wanted to do in this life."

Ayanna stared at him, and there was no mistaking his sincerity. "But, Johnny, you didn't mess anything up. I did. I thought so little of myself that it just didn't occur to me that you really cared about me. I couldn't see that you couldn't have treated me the way you did unless you had real feelings for me. I just took your love and tossed it in your face," she said sadly. "I'm the one who should be begging your pardon. I couldn't see clearly what I had done until my mother and Billie got me straight," she said. "I hope you can forgive me."

Johnny came over to her side of the booth and kissed her. "Ayanna, angel, don't ever apologize to me again. We both made mistakes. We both acted hastily, and we won't ever do it again. I promise you that from my heart," he said.

They were deep into a long, soul-healing kiss when a voice brought them back to the present.

"Y'all don't really want this, do you? I can bring it back, 'cause y'all look a little busy." It was their server, a gangly college kid named Keyshawn. He was holding a tray of cheeseburgers, onion rings and two cherry colas, and he looked vastly amused.

Ayanna giggled and put her head in the crook of Johnny's neck.

"Hey, I'm starving, and she needs to eat, so put it right here, partner. Sorry for the show," Johnny said, but he didn't sound sorry in the least.

"Hey, no problem. Now I know I have something to look forward to when I get…um, out of school," Keyshawn said as he unloaded the tray. "Enjoy your meal," he added.

"Was he about to call me old? I know he wasn't going to call me old, fine as I am," Johnny mumbled.

"You're gorgeous. Now eat. I can hear your stomach growling from here," Ayanna said.

"By the way, Celeste signed that book for you."

Ayanna eagerly looked for the inscription that read, "This book was handed to you by the man who will love you the rest of your lives. Be good to him and to yourself. Hugs, Celeste."

They went back to the hospital and held hands and talked all night, until all the pain was a thing of the past.

When the time for visiting hours arrived, Johnny was allowed to go in to see Cameron. Ayanna was touched to her heart to see tears in his eyes when he came out.

"He's going to be fine, Ayanna. God's not going to take him from us, I promise you." He held her tight and they prayed together.

"It's about time you got here." The voice was Lucie's. She held out her arms for a hug, which Johnny gladly gave her.

"Sorry it took so long, but I was in England," he said.

"You're here now, that's all that matters. How is my grandson this morning?"

Ayanna said sadly, "There doesn't seem to be any change, Mommy."

Lucie took her hand and held her tightly. "Don't sound so sad, honey. When there seems to be no change it isn't a bad thing, Ayanna. He's stable, which is better than him taking a sharp turn for the worse. I'm going to talk to the nurse, I'll be right back."

While Lucie went to pry information out of the charge nurse, Lee and Boyd Phillips showed up. Lee went to Ayanna and held her tight. "Ayanna, darling girl, we've been praying for you and the boys. I'm not going to get in the way, but I had to be here with you. How are you holding up?"

"I'm fine now," Ayanna said. "I can't believe you came all the way from Pittsburgh just to see about us," she said tearfully.

"You're family," Boyd said gruffly. "Now don't start crying again. I had three women in my house that would cry at the drop of a hat. Please don't start," he pleaded.

"I'll try," she promised. Turning to Johnny, she said, "Johnny, I'm going to be here the rest of the day, so you might want to get some rest." Lucie came back in time to hear her.

"No, you're not going to stay here. Johnny, please take her home. She left here yesterday for the first time since Cameron was admitted, and she was right back here six hours later. She's been here over twelve hours now, and she needs some rest." She looked at Lee and Boyd and said, "You must be Johnny's parents. I'm sorry to sound like a shrew, but my daughter doesn't like taking my advice. She really does need some rest."

Lee agreed. "Johnny, get our girl out of here, and don't let her come back for a good long time. We can hold down the fort here."

Johnny agreed with her. "Come on, sweetness. I'm taking you home."

In a couple of hours, Ayanna was in bed in a way she thought was a thing of the past. She was curled up next to Johnny, feeling the warmth of his embrace. When they got to her house, they took a shower and went to bed. Even without making love, the contact was intimate and reassuring.

"I thought you hated me," she whispered.

"I could never, ever hate you. You're too precious to me. You are the other half of my heart," he said with a huge yawn.

"That was romantic," she giggled. "Can you show a little more interest, please?"

"Just as soon as I wake up, I'll show you all the interest you can handle," he promised.

He went to sleep almost immediately, but Ayanna stayed awake for a while. Despite her joy at being reunited with Johnny, she couldn't close her eyes. She was too consumed with Cameron's condition. She finally drifted off and slept surprisingly well in Johnny's arms.

A phone call woke them, and Ayanna's heart leapt into her throat. "Johnny, we have to get to the hospital. There's been a change."

Ayanna wasn't sure her legs would support her as they rounded the corner to the intensive care unit. Lucie, Lee and Boyd were waiting for her, and so was the doctor.

"There has been a profound change in his condition," the doctor said. "The medication is taking hold and the infection is clearing up. It looks like he won't need surgery after all."

Tears of joy ran down her face as Johnny wrapped his arms around her. "Can I see him, please?"

When she went into the unit, she felt a thrill like no other as Cameron looked at her sleepily. "Ma, I'm hungry. What do I have to do to get some real food?"

This time her tears were from nothing but joy and gratitude.

Chapter 19

"John, I'm ready to go home. When can I get out of here?"

Cameron was out of intensive care, and Todd and his other doctors had assured Ayanna that his release was imminent. Johnny smiled at his eagerness.

"Cam, you're going home tomorrow if all your tests come back clean. Just chill and enjoy taking it easy for one more day."

"I'll chill when I get home. I miss being at home with Ma and Alec," Cameron countered. "Being stuck here is not 'taking it easy.' I have a lot of homework to make up, and besides, Ma's been missing work, and she's had a whole bunch to deal with me being sick and all. When

I'm home she'll know I'm well, and she can relax for a change."

Johnny was surprised to hear Cameron speak with such maturity. He knew more about Ayanna than she realized, he thought. He was shocked at Cameron's next words.

"She doesn't know this, but I know what happened to my mother and father. I heard Aunt Emily talking about it to one of her friends. My dad wasn't such a good man. I can remember him yelling and screaming at my mother a lot," Cameron said solemnly. "He used to hit her, and when he started hitting us, she said she was leaving and going back to Grandma. And then one night neither one of them came home. Ma and Grandma came to get us and told us there had been a car accident. But I heard what Aunt Emily said about what Dad did."

Johnny prayed for guidance and moved his chair closer to Cameron's bed. "Cam, your dad wasn't well," he began.

"I know that," Cameron said. "He had to be sick in the head to do what he did. But I don't want to be like him, so I try to do what Ma tells me to do and to be a good man." He was silent for a moment, and then looked Johnny in the eye, man-to-man.

"You know, she never went out before she met you. Alec and I think you're a good man, John. You're the kind of guy she should be with."

"I try to be a good man, Cameron. And I can promise you that I would never mistreat your mother in any way.

I've never gotten physical with a woman in my life, and I never would. Especially not your mom. She's very special to me."

Cameron was fiddling with his PSP as they talked. His thumbs stopped moving, and he raised an eyebrow. "You love her, don't you?"

"Yes, I do. I love her with all my heart."

"Good. You made a good choice, John. She can cook, she's very tidy and she can refinish furniture. And she's very thrifty, too. She won't waste your money, that's for sure. My mom is tight with a buck," he said ruefully.

Ayanna came into the hospital room looking more rested and less harried. Alec was with her, carrying one of her bakery-style boxes. Johnny stood up when she entered and kissed her on the cheek. "What are you guys talking about?" She kissed her son on the forehead.

"Man stuff, Ma. What did you bring me to eat?"

"You act like they're starving you, sweetie."

"They may as well," he said mournfully. "The food here sucks."

"It really does. The cafeteria food even sucks," Alec agreed.

"Cameron and Alec, what have I told you about that word?" Ayanna sounded amused and exasperated at the same time.

"Sorry, Ma." Cameron grinned. "The food here isn't as palatable as your cuisine. How's that?"

"Better. You can have your chocolate chip and peanut butter cookies now."

"Cool beans!" He gleefully took the box from Alec.

Johnny put his arms around Ayanna and hugged her. Everything was getting back to normal, but if he had his way, everything would change again—this time for the better. At least he hoped it would.

In a couple of weeks it was just like nothing had happened. Cameron had spent some time at home before he was considered well enough to go back to school. The school had been completely sanitized after the officials realized there was a MRSA infection. Lucie had taken vacation time so she was able to stay with Ayanna and the boys. As Johnny suspected, Lucie and his mother, Lee, got along like long-lost sisters, and they thoroughly enjoyed each other's company.

Ayanna went back to work and promised Nick that she'd make up the time she'd taken off for Cameron's illness. Nick had looked at her like she was crazy.

"Ayanna, don't even try it. You're family, girl. Call it sick leave, compassionate leave, FMLA or whatever you want, but don't try and make it up. Your child was sick. What were you supposed to do but take care of him?" He walked off muttering, and that was the end of it. Ayanna already knew she was blessed, but his response made her realize how lucky she was. A lot of employers would have fired her for missing so much time, but he wouldn't even let her try to make up the time off.

She was too blessed to be stressed, as the saying went. One of the best things was having Johnny back in her life. When he had come to her in the hospital, it was like waking up from a coma. He had dropped everything and flown home from another country to be with her in her time of need. She didn't need any more proof than that to know he really cared about her and about her boys and that was all that mattered.

They didn't have a lot of time together, what with her mother and his parents in town and Cameron coming home, but the time they did have was precious to her. But it was wonderful having everyone around, too. She felt like part of a really big happy family. For so long it had been just her mother, her sister and the boys, and now she felt like she was part of a loving community. Johnny surprised her one day by asking how she felt about families.

"Do you ever want to get married and have more children?"

They were on the screened porch of her house, stealing a minute to say good-night before he went to his borrowed apartment. It caught her off guard but she answered him honestly.

"Yes, Johnny, I do. I want to get married and have some babies. At least two," she said firmly.

"So you like big families? All the commotion and racket and people getting in each other's business, that doesn't bother you?" he asked curiously.

"Not at all," she replied. "I love it, in fact. You seem to thrive on it, why wouldn't I?"

"Some people prefer their privacy," he said mildly.

"'The grave's a fine and private place,'" she quoted.

"Life is for the living, and after what I've been through I'll take as much as I can get."

"I see," he said thoughtfully. He cupped his hands around her face. "I love this face. It's beautiful," he whispered.

"I love you," she said softly.

"I have to go back to the brothel," he said. That was the name he'd given the apartment. "You know, if you'd help me find a house I wouldn't have to stay there," he reminded her.

"Well, if I had a better idea of what you wanted, I could," she retorted.

"That's easy. A big brick house with enough room for four or five kids and a wife." He watched her face change as she digested this information.

"Sounds like you're a man with a plan," she said slowly.

"I am," he agreed.

"It's about time," she said saucily and moaned as Johnny kissed the smile right off her face.

That Friday Cameron begged for a special dinner. He wanted a lasagna dinner, and he wanted everyone to come. "Please, Ma? This way I can say thank you to Miss Billie and Miss Dakota and Mr. Hunter and everybody. Everybody was so nice when I was sick, and now I can thank everyone personally," he explained.

Ayanna was so touched that she agreed at once. Lucie thought it was a brilliant, wonderful idea, and the two of them started cooking. It was a big party and required a big menu. They decided on antipasto and bruschetta for appetizers, lasagna, spaghetti and eggplant parmigiana for the main courses and a huge green salad. There would be lots of garlic bread, wine for the adults and juice for the children and gelato, tiramisu and cannoli for dessert. Billie and Dakota insisted on contributing, even though Lucie and Ayanna said it wasn't necessary.

It was a casual affair, so Ayanna didn't understand Lucie's insistence that she look her best, but she did take special care in her attire. She wore a pretty summer dress with a gold shimmer and cap sleeves to show off her arms and a wide gold belt to show off her waist. The skirt of the dress was wide and flared out around her knees so her legs were on display, too. She applied makeup like she was going out on the town, just to appease Lucie.

"Oh, you look so pretty, sweetie pie," Lucie said.

"Mommy, I wish Emily had come," Ayanna said. "We used to be so tight, but now she acts like we're strangers."

Lucie nodded. "She'll come around eventually, I'm sure. But let's worry about the ones who are here, not the ones who couldn't make it, okay?"

Ayanna saw the wisdom of her mother's words as their guests arrived. Nick and Dakota and Bethany, Toni and Zane and little Brandon, Lee and Boyd Phillips, Billie and Jason, Todd, Cameron's friends Zack and Anthony and their parents and more filled the house. The food was superb, the company was joyful and the evening was so much fun that Ayanna wasn't surprised when Johnny proposed a toast.

"To our lovely hostesses, thanks for an amazing feast. To Cameron, who came up with the brilliant idea of bringing everyone together tonight. And to my parents, who raised me right," he said.

Ayanna tilted her head slightly when she heard that. He was standing behind her with his arm around her waist, so she couldn't see his expression, but she thought it was an odd direction for the toast to take.

"I'm really happy that all our friends and family were able to be here for this occasion," he said. "Those of you who know me well know that it sometimes takes me a long time to decide what's best for me, but once I make that decision, nothing changes my mind. It didn't take me long to realize that Ayanna is the best thing that ever happened to me, but I took my own stupid time to let her know that."

Ayanna's mouth opened, and she covered it with her hand. Johnny turned her to face him and spoke directly to her. "I love you with all my heart, and I want to ask you if you'll be kind enough to marry me so I can spend the rest of my life taking care of you and Alec and Cameron and all the beautiful babies I hope we have in the future. Will you please say yes?"

Without hesitation, she said, "Absolutely. I love you." They kissed to a chorus of cheers and applause. Alec and Cameron were smiling from ear to ear as he slipped a three-carat diamond solitaire on her ring finger.

"This is some serious mushy stuff," Alec said.

"Yeah, but it's way cool, too," Cameron replied.

Chapter 20

The next logical step in the process of becoming a family was finding a house and planning a wedding. Ayanna was stunned to find out that Jason had the perfect property, located about three blocks from where he and Billie lived.

"I've had my eye on it, and I figured it would be perfect once you guys got your stuff in order," he said. "It has six bedrooms, three and a half baths, a study, a media room, a four-car garage and a laundry room on the second floor. Plus," he added, smiling at Ayanna, "the previous owner was a gourmet chef. The kitchen is stupendous. Wait until you see it," he assured her. "You'll love it."

It was indeed an amazing house. Lucie, Alec and

Cameron loved it immediately, and Johnny was ready to close the deal as soon as he saw it. Lee and Boyd had already seen it and thought it was perfect. Ayanna went from room to room in awe, trying to calculate the monthly upkeep and the mortgage on a house of that size. She was almost completely silent on the way home, something that Johnny noticed at once. After Alec and Cameron went to bed and Lucie went to the study for her nightly CNN fix, he talked to her about the house.

"Didn't you like it?" he asked.

"I thought it was wonderful, Johnny, but it's so expensive! Can we afford it?"

"Absolutely," he assured her. "First of all, it's not as pricey as you might think. The previous owner moved to California to open a restaurant, and he wants to sell fast because he needs the money. In the second place, I never intended to live in a condo or an apartment the rest of my life. I have money put aside for a home. In the third place, I may not be as frugal as you, but I don't waste money, either. I have some good investments. My mom's hobby is investing. She started a club about ten years ago with a few of her friends, and those women know the market better than a lot of brokers. We'll never be broke."

They were on her sofa with her in his lap while he kissed her neck and reassured her. "By the way, you never did put these on," he reminded her. He pulled the pearl and diamond earrings out of his pants pocket and presented them to her again.

"You're so sweet to me. What am I going to do with you?"

"Let me kidnap you," he replied.

"Kidnap me? Are you serious?"

"I am. Before Lucie and my folks go home, I want to take you away for the weekend. Have you ever heard of French Lick?"

Ayanna gave him a seductive smile. "Didn't you do that to me a few times?" She collapsed in laughter while he tickled her.

"Yes, yes, I've heard of French Lick, Indiana. There's a resort and a casino there," she gasped. "Did I ever tell you how ticklish I am?"

"That's good to know," he answered. "But yeah, there's a really nice resort and spa and casino and stuff, and I want to take you there for the weekend. It'll be the last time we have any time together before the wedding, so let's take advantage of it. Please say you'll be my willing hostage," he whispered as he rimmed her ear with his tongue.

"Keep doing that, and I'll agree to anything."

French Lick was everything Johnny said it was and more. They arrived on Saturday morning, and Ayanna was awed by everything she saw. The French Lick Springs Hotel was an amazing place, built in the 1800s and recently restored to its original grandeur. The grounds were magnificent, as well as the lavishly ornate lobby. Their room was so sinfully comfortable that Ayanna didn't want to budge, but Johnny reminded her of the spa experience that awaited her.

"They have this special mineral water that's supposed to make you feel fantastic."

"I read about it. It's called Pluto water, and it used to be sold as a laxative," she said.

"Okay, that's just nasty."

"If you really needed one, you wouldn't think so," she said cheerily. She was across the bed, still fully dressed.

He pounced on her, and they wrestled playfully. "The purpose of this weekend is not to talk about digestive problems. We're supposed to be relaxing, rejuvenating and releasing, or did you forget?"

"You're right. Lead me to the spa."

Four hours later, she came back to the room in a state of bliss. Her skin looked and felt like silk, and she felt like a million dollars. There was a note on the pillow that read "Take a nap, sweetheart. I decided to get a massage, too. See you soon. Love you."

Ayanna got undressed and slipped into the soft comfortable bed, falling into a deep sleep almost instantly. She slept for three hours, until she was wakened by the warmth of Johnny's hand stroking her back. Smiling sleepily, she turned in his direction and invited him to join her.

"Nope. If I get in there with you I'm not getting out until an hour before we leave to go home. We're going to have a really nice dinner, and then I'm going to do something I've never done with you before."

She propped herself up on one elbow. "What's that?"

"We've never danced together, and I'm going to remedy that tonight."

It was the sweetest thing she'd ever heard. "What in the world am I going to wear?"

Johnny gave her his familiar, endearing smile. "How about this?" he asked, holding up a garment bag.

It was an ivory dress in silk, cut on the bias so it would cling to her body. It had wide-set straps that crossed in the back and a skirt that would swirl around her knees when she moved. It was truly the sexiest dress she could ever remember owning. There was also sheer underwear to go with it, a bustier and thong in a café-au-lait shade that matched her skin. She was enchanted with what she saw.

"Did you pick out all by yourself?"

"I did," he said proudly. "Lucie gave me the sizes, and I went for it."

"I can't wait to put them on," she said. "You have good taste. Excellent taste, really."

"I sure do. I picked you, didn't I?"

Ayanna looked fabulous in the dress. The bodice of the dress dipped low with a sexy drape that showed an enticing bit of cleavage. She was shimmering from an artful application of gold powder here and there, and she smelled of her usual Chanel No. 5. Even her feet looked sexy in gold sandals. She touched her earlobe and smiled. The chocolate diamonds sparkled, and the pearls seemed to make her face glow. Her hair was blown out and curled, and it was evident that it was growing out because it touched the back of her neck. It was very becoming in a tousled, sexy style. She turned around to see if Johnny approved of her ensemble, and her breath caught in her throat. He looked so handsome she couldn't say a word.

He was wearing a custom-tailored suit in a heavenly shade of brown with an ivory shirt and matching silk tie. His dark chiseled features stood out against the ivory, and his meticulously barbered mustache and goatee were impeccable. She was staring at him so intensely he thought something was amiss.

"Is my tie crooked?"

"No, it's perfect. My goodness, we're going to have the most amazing sons," she said in a hushed voice.

"I already have two amazing sons. I want a couple of sweet little girls," he said. "Stay right there, I have to do something."

Ayanna stood patiently while Johnny's masculine scent wafted over her. She was acutely aware of his nearness, so much so that she didn't feel the necklace until he fastened the clasp. She touched it before looking at it in the mirror. "Oh, Johnny, it's beautiful! It matches my earrings."

The delicate gold chain with the large chocolate pearl and the sparkling chocolate diamonds made her want to cry, but she held it in. "This is the most beautiful thing I've ever seen."

"Then I did really good because it's on the most beautiful woman in the world. Let's get out of here before I lose my mind."

Ayanna was reluctant to leave because the only thing she was hungry for was Johnny, but she went with him to the restaurant. She was glad they did because the food was lovely. It was well-prepared and a treat for the eye as well as the palate. She had a petite filet that was pink in the middle—just the way she liked it. It was served with a little cup of sorbet to refresh the palate between bites so that each bite would taste like the first. It was served with wild rice pilaf and *haricots verts*, the slender French green beans that were so tender they melted in the mouth. Johnny had chosen an excellent wine, and she was having such a wonderful time that she never wanted the evening to end.

But Johnny was serious about dancing. "Did you enjoy your meal?"

"Did you see me try to lick the plate? Yes, I did, it was delicious. How was yours?"

"Not as good as your cooking, but it was tasty. Now then, my lady, I think you owe me a dance."

They went to the casino, which was as lively as Vegas, but classier. The neoclassical style of the architecture and the extraordinary high ceilings gave it a certain elegance and grandeur. The jazz band was playing a Latin number when they entered, and Johnny took Ayanna out on the dance floor. She was by far the best partner he'd ever danced with. He'd known a lot of women who thought they could dance, but Ayanna could burn up the floor.

At one point they literally cleared the floor, and people stood and watched them execute their moves like they'd been dancing together forever. They had to take a bow because everyone applauded like mad.

"I'm ready for a breather if you are," Ayanna told Johnny.

"Of course, sweetness." They went to a table and Johnny ordered Perrier water for both of them. "There's some champagne on ice in the room, but if you want something stronger now, go ahead."

"This is wonderful. You've been holding out on me. You're a wonderful dancer," she told him.

"I get around on the floor, but damn, Ayanna, you float. We're going to throw down at our wedding."

Ayanna looked at her sparkling ring, loving the weight of it on her delicate finger. "Johnny, this wedding is going to break us," she said worriedly. "Even a small wedding with about seventy-five people can cost about twenty thousand dollars when you factor in food and drinks and flowers and invitations and favors."

Johnny laughed at her softly. He leaned over to kiss her. "Sweetness, when are you going to realize that I got this? Your job from now on is not to worry about anything. And you can forget about eloping. Your family, my family, our extended family and our boys all want a celebration."

Ayanna smiled and kissed him. "Okay, okay, okay. But I want everything pink, and I want you to wear a white tux and a pink ruffled shirt."

The look on his face was without a doubt the funniest thing she'd ever seen, and they were still laughing when they strolled through the casino on their way back to their room. "Wait a minute, Johnny. I've always wanted to play one of these."

They stopped next to a ten-dollar slot machine, and she pulled out a crisp new bill. She kissed it for luck and fed it into the one-armed bandit. She pulled the long shiny metal arm and watched the cylinders spin around and around. "I should have kept my ten bucks," she murmured.

Suddenly buzzers and lights started going off and the noise seemed deafening. "What happened?" she asked Johnny.

"You just won the jackpot, baby, that's what happened."

"Wow. Cool beans," she said with a grin just like Cameron's.

Chapter 21

The jackpot was almost two hundred thousand dollars. Ayanna was giddy but contained it when they got back to their room. "You're going to have to remind me tomorrow that this happened," she said. "I don't think it's really real."

Johnny laughed as he took off his tie. "It's real, baby. You are now a moderately comfortable woman," he teased her.

"We are a fortunate family," she corrected him. "What's mine is yours. And what's yours is mine, and I want to see it," she said seductively.

"See what?"

"Skin. Take off your jacket, please."

"If you take off your shoes," he countered. "I love your little feet."

She took off one shoe and dangled it from her little finger. "Your turn."

He obligingly removed the jacket. "Other shoe, please."

She took the other one off, and then she tucked her feet under her skirt. "Shirt, please."

He pulled it out of his waistband and unbuttoned it.

"All the way off," Ayanna insisted.

He removed it, and she sighed when she saw his rippling muscles. "You're way too sexy."

"No, that's you, baby. Take off that pretty dress for me."

"This isn't coming out right. You have on more clothes than me. Take off those shoes and socks," she demanded.

"If it'll make you happy," he said as he kicked off his expensive Italian shoes and sat down to remove his socks.

"I need help," Ayanna purred. She rose to her knees and turned so he could unfasten her dress. Once the straps were undone he slid the zipper down, blowing softly on her back as he did so.

She was now wearing nothing but the seductive lingerie and her jewelry. She didn't have to say anything about his pants because he took them off with a quickness, along with his briefs. "Oh, now I'm over-dressed," Ayanna said.

"Leave that on," Johnny said. "You look amazing."

In seconds they were under the covers, kissing like they'd been apart for a year. They were hungry for each other, starving for the sensations they could only get in each other's arms. Their lips caressed, and their tongues met and mated over and over again while their hands explored passion-heated skin.

"Johnny, take it off. I need you to touch me," she whispered.

He was already rubbing her breasts but she wanted more. He unhooked the front clasp and freed her so he could do what she wanted him to do. He licked the tender spot between her breasts and started massaging one erect nipple with his fingers while he sucked the other.

"Mmm, Johnny," she moaned.

His other hand was palming her behind, squeezing and rubbing until the flesh was dampened with perspiration. He moved his mouth to her other breast and his hand to the juncture of her thighs, which was already wet from her desire. She climaxed almost immediately, and he could feel the tremors rippling through her body. He kept kissing her, going down her torso until his mouth could bestow the most intimate kiss possible. She tasted so good he could have stayed there forever drinking in her sweetness. The way she moved her hips when she came, the sounds she uttered were so arousing that he didn't want to stop, but she pleaded with him.

"I need you inside me right now, Johnny, right now," she moaned.

He didn't hesitate to give her just what she wanted. He joined their bodies in a smooth, easy motion that turned into a wild coupling that brought her over the brink again and again. He wanted to make sure she was satisfied before he let the silky heat of her body take him away. When she tightened on him and said his name with so much tenderness, he fell in love with her all over again and finally let go. He moaned out her name as his orgasm took over his body. He thrust his manhood into her sweetness one last time, holding her so tight their hearts beat as one.

They drove back to Chicago with dreamy smiles on their faces. "We were supposed to go horseback riding, you know."

Ayanna looked over at Johnny and rubbed her free hand on his muscular forearm. Her other hand was holding his. "I didn't want to ride a horse," she said.

"We could have gone on a tour," he pointed out.

"I saw everything I wanted to see," she answered.

They looked at each other and smiled again.

"You'd better wipe that smile off your face before Lucie sees you or she's going to know what we've been up to," he cautioned her.

"Honey, once we tell her about that jackpot she won't give a rip. We could tell her we robbed a bank and she wouldn't care. Our moms can plan the wedding of the century for all I care. And we can get the house and lots of furniture, too."

"And you can quit your job. If you want to," he said.

"I can what?"

"You don't have to work anymore, if you don't want

to. I make enough to support us all. You can go to culinary school and open those restaurants the way you planned. How does that sound?"

"It sounds like something I never thought about," she admitted.

"Start thinking about it, Ayanna. I want you to be happy. From now on, you and Alec and Cameron are my priority, my only priority. I want you to be happy and safe and protected, and that also goes for all those little girls we're going to have."

"You really want little girls? Most men want boys."

"I told you, I have two fine sons already. If we have more, that's fine. But you've seen how cute Bethany is. Just imagine what our baby will look like. Sweet and pretty and adorable, just like her cousin. You must admit that seeing Nick with Bethany is something else."

"She has him wrapped around her tiny little finger, that's for sure. And you want that, too, don't you?"

"Absolutely. She'll look just like you, and she'll be smart like Cameron and Alec and funny like me."

"Johnny, you've given this an amazing amount of thought," she said.

"Just since I met you. When I was a litigator in labor law, I used to spend a lot of time thinking about my clients and preparing a case. I guess the habit carried over," he admitted.

"So you've been preparing for a case, is that it?"

"The biggest one of my life. This was a case for love, baby. I had to win."

"You did, on all counts."

* * *

Ayanna gave in to her mother and future mother-in-law and let them plan the wedding of their dreams. Money was literally no object, and they went nuts, but she was too happy to care. Johnny had no preferences except for the theme. He surprised them all when he said he wanted it to be "Diamonds and Pearls." "Because my wife is a true diamond and her skin is as smooth as a perfect pearl. Because that's the first real gift I gave her and because that's going to be the song we dance to at the reception," he explained. The women were in the living room of the new house, arranging furniture and making plans.

"You can do whatever else you want as long as it's diamonds and pearls. You can have dancing monkeys, singing frogs and a marching band if you want. Oh, and the groom's cake must be red velvet." He left the room singing the Prince tune and looking perfectly happy.

"That's an amazing young man," Lucie said.

Lee smiled at her. "He's my son, and I love him, but he's a crazy young man. Well, 'Diamonds and Pearls' it is then."

They worked like crazy to create a beautiful day for Johnny and Ayanna, who really appreciated everything they were doing. They kept her in the loop and consulted with her on various things, but for the most part, they had carte blanche. It was going to be a Christmas wedding, and Ayanna was sure it would be beautiful. Her main concern was getting the house ready for them to move into.

Johnny was supportive and surprisingly helpful. He patiently went over color charts with her; he went furniture shopping and let her know what he liked. With Billie and Dakota and Toni helping her, she was really pleased with her choices, especially in the master bedroom.

The walls were a soothing shade of robin's-egg blue and with ivory crown molding and the silk bedding was chocolate-brown and pale blue. The bed was so big she needed a set of steps to get in and out, but it was the right size for a big man like Johnny. The furniture wasn't too masculine or feminine, and the teak stain went beautifully with the colors she'd chosen.

The boys selected their own colors for their bedrooms. They were bouncing off the walls with excitement, even when Lucie told them they were going to be in the wedding. Johnny had asked if they could be part of the ceremony as he committed himself to their mother. "I wanted them to be a part of it, because this is going to make us a family," he said. The formal adoption would be after New Year's, but he wanted them to feel included from the very beginning.

By Thanksgiving everything was set except for the maid of honor. Emily had been acting as though she didn't care whether or not she participated, and Ayanna couldn't stand it anymore. She called Emily the week before Thanksgiving and told her point-blank that if she didn't come to Chicago with Lucie for Thanksgiving she would assume that Emily had better things to do than be her maid of honor.

"You're my baby sister, and I've loved you since the day you were born. I've always tried to be there for you even when you've made it plain that you don't want to be bothered with me. But this is it, Emmie. I'm through begging you to be a part of my life. It's time to fish or cut bait. If you're not here for Thanksgiving, I'll know your answer," Ayanna said.

After the call, she fretted, thinking that she'd pushed too hard. But when Lucie arrived for the holiday, Emily came, too. Ayanna was overcome with joy and hugged her sister tightly.

"Just don't put me in something frilly and stupid," she muttered. "I'd look like a lumberjack in drag."

She had no worries on that score. Toni had found a shop with an amazing array of styles. Ayanna had chosen a simple, elegant dress for the bridesmaids. The dresses were café au lait with ivory sashes, except for Emily's—she would be wearing the colors in reverse. She annoyed everyone by not letting anyone see her dress until the wedding day. Even Lucie hadn't seen it.

"I know my daughter has good taste, but this is killing me," she confided to Lee. "She picked the darndest time to start being mysterious."

Lee commiserated with her. "At least she let us put on a big wedding. Nick and Dakota had that little ceremony at their house! It was wonderful, but she was my oldest daughter, and I wanted something big and lavish like Billie's wedding, doggone it."

"Well, she made up for it, Lee. You have the prettiest little grandbaby in the world. And pretty soon, we'll have some more. I have a feeling that Ayanna and Johnny are going to make some beauties."

"And you know this, girl!" Lee held up her hand for a high five.

The wedding took place the day after Christmas. It snowed during the night, and everything looked like a beautiful Christmas card. The trees and shrubs were coated with sparkling white, and everything looked pure and pristine. The limousines hired for the wedding party were white, too, and they made a very elegant appearance as they pulled up to the church. The bridesmaids were all dressed before they arrived at church. Ayanna was already there, getting dressed with only Toni to assist her.

Toni's blue eyes filled with tears as she looked at Ayanna. "Thank goodness for waterproof mascara. You look amazing, girl."

"Thank you, Toni. And thank you for helping pick out the dress and keeping it a secret. I just want to wow everybody. I have no idea why," she murmured.

"Because you can. You're the bride, it's your day. Knock 'em dead, toots! I've got to go get in the line. See you soon!"

Toni went to join the other bridesmaids, and Ayanna said a silent prayer. Taking a deep breath, she opened the dressing room door. When her maid of honor, Emily, entered the church, it was Ayanna's cue. She went into the hallway and waited until the wedding coordinator opened the door, and she began her walk down the aisle to Johnny.

She had debated about having her mother escort her, or Jason or even Todd, but in the end she decided to go it alone. No one was giving her away to Johnny; she was giving herself, freely and lovingly. Her friends and family all rose to watch her walk down the aisle, but she couldn't really see them. Her eyes were fixed firmly on Johnny, on her future.

A collective "ooh" rose as she walked gracefully down the aisle. Her dress looked like it was made of diamonds and pearls. It was a creamy white with a halter neck and a fitted bodice to show off her curves. The bottom of the dress was a column with a split in the front and a train in the back. It was made entirely of lace with hundreds of pearls and crystals that caught the light like little twinkling stars. She carried a bouquet of creamy white and green orchids, and she had smaller orchids in her hair.

Johnny looked like a prince in his elegant black suit. He wore an ivory shirt and ivory silk tie, as did his best man, his father, and all the groomsmen. Alec and Cameron looked so grown up she wanted to cry. But there were no tears during the ceremony, at least not from Johnny and Ayanna. Their smiles were constant and full of the joy they felt. Ayanna had to dab her eyes with her grandmother's lace hanky when the minister asked Alec and Cameron to come forward and Johnny said the words that bound them as family. He gave them each a gold bracelet to wear and they gave him one. Ayanna wanted to weep, but from what she could hear, Lee and Lucie were doing enough of that for the whole family.

When the minister pronounced them man and wife they kissed each other, briefly and sweetly. When he pronounced them a family, they all hugged. It was a moment she'd never forget as long as she lived.

The reception was held at a big hotel in downtown Chicago, and it was the best party she'd ever attended, bar none. The ballroom looked like a fantasy come to life. There were tall crystal vases with orchids and calla lilies submerged in water supporting branches of crystals and white roses. The table settings looked like they belonged in a palace, and the cakes were amazing. The wedding cake was covered with edible pearls and sugar crystals, and it looked like some royal baker had done it for a king and queen.

When she and Johnny took the dance floor for their first dance she looked up at him with her heart in her eyes. "I'm not going to wake up, am I? We're really truly man and wife, aren't we?"

"Oh yes, sweetness. For the rest of out lives, we're together." He looked over at Alec and Cameron, who were dancing on the sidelines. "All of us."

Epilogue

"I hope you're happy," Ayanna said sleepily.

"I'm ecstatic," Johnny told her.

"Next time I tell you I'm in labor, I'll bet you'll believe me, won't you?" They had barely made it to the hospital before she delivered.

Johnny laughed softly and kissed his beautiful wife.

"Sweetheart, I'll never doubt you again." He was sitting on the side of their bed, holding a tiny beauty with a head of thick black curls.

"Which one do you have?"

"I have Madison. Your mother has Lindsey," he told her.

"No, your mother has Lindsey, and I've come for Madison," Lucie informed them. "Come see Grandma,

sweetie," she cooed as she took the sleeping infant.
She hummed happily as she left the room.

"Come lie down with me," Ayanna said softly. "I
want my husband."

"You've got me, sweetness." He put his arms around
her and held her close to his heart. "How did you manage
to have twins nine months to the day after we got
married and still be the sexiest woman I've ever
known?"

She cuddled closer to him. "You need glasses."

He stroked her hair, which was much longer and
thicker. "You're my beauty and always will be."

Ayanna's eyes were closed, and he knew she'd be
asleep in a minute. She was so amazing. Billie, Dakota
and Toni were all appalled when she never had a day
of morning sickness. She didn't even get fat; she just
got really big breasts and a huge belly, which he found
incredibly sexy. Every day and every way she was a
total source of joy and happiness for him.

He'd had to change jobs and found a better-paying
position with a firm based in Chicago because he
couldn't handle being away from her and their sons.
She was worth any change he'd made, any sacrifice at
all because in her arms he was whole. She made his life
complete. And now she'd given him not one but two
little girls. She was going to flip out when she saw the
diamond earrings he'd bought her and the babies, but
she'd get over it.

He kissed her forehead and listened to her peaceful,
even breathing before joining her in sleep.

REQUEST YOUR FREE BOOKS!

2 FREE NOVELS
PLUS 2 FREE GIFTS!

KIMANI™ ROMANCE

Love's ultimate destination!

KROM0

**A mistake from the past
ignites a fiery future….**

NEW YORK TIMES BESTSELLING AUTHOR

BRENDA JACKSON

FIRE AND DESIRE

A Madaris Family Novel

When Corinthians Avery snuck into a hotel room to seduce
Dex Madaris, it was Trevor Grant who emerged from the
shower to find her wearing next to nothing, and informed
her Dex was at home, happily married.

Two years later, traveling with Trevor on business,
Corinthians tries to avoid him, but his sexy smile sets her
on fire. And when a dangerous situation arises, they find
fear turning to feverish desire, never realizing that one
passionate night will change their lives forever….

*Available the first week of January 2009
wherever books are sold.*

ARABESQUE®

**www.kimanipress.com
www.myspace.com/kimanipress**

KPBJ0540109

NATIONAL BESTSELLING AUTHOR

ROCHELLE ALERS

invites you to meet the Whitfields of New York....

Tessa, Faith and Simone Whitfield know all about coordinating
other people's weddings, and not so much about arranging
their own love lives. But in the space of one unforgettable year,
all three will meet intriguing men who just might bring them their
very own happily ever after....

Long Time Coming

June 2008

The Sweetest Temptation

July 2008

Taken by Storm

August 2008

ARABESQUE®

www.kimanipress.com